TRA

Presented to

Jenny

christmas

1996

from

St. Marks

G.F.S.

VALLEY BOOKS, MONMOUTH, GWENT.

Tracy and the Warriors

LYNDA NEILANDS

KINGSWAY PUBLICATIONS

EASTBOURNE

Front cover design by Vic Mitchell

British Library Cataloguing in Publication Data

Neilands, Lynda
Tracy and the warriors.
I. Title
823.914 [J]

ISBN 0–86065–857–0

Printed in Great Britain for
KINGSWAY PUBLICATIONS LTD
1 St Anne's Road, Eastbourne, E Sussex BN21 3UN by
Richard Clay Ltd, Bungay, Suffolk.
Typeset by J&L Composition Ltd, Filey, North Yorkshire.

To Christopher and Patrick

CHAPTER ONE

Tracy MacArthur sat on the doorstep of her Glasgow home, her chin between her knees. Behind her the pink-papered hallway was stuffed to overflowing. Suitcases and equipment, neatly tagged with Ugandan Airline luggage labels, bulged through the front door, while her own wellington boots and rucksack jammed the narrow passage to the kitchen.

In six hours' time she would catch the ferry to Ireland to spend a month at her aunt's. She sighed deeply, longing for some last-minute change of plan. If only she could jet off to Uganda with her parents instead. She had never even met Auntie Nadia. And Ireland was bound to be wet. How could anyone look forward to a holiday with unknown relatives in the rain?

'Let me come with you ... please!' she pleaded again as her mother squeezed past.

'I'm sorry, darling,' Mrs MacArthur replied brightly. 'Between eye clinics and water projects your dad and I will be travelling non-stop. You really will be safer this way—and happier. And your cousin, Peter, is only four years older than you are. The time will fly past, you'll see.'

Ten seconds ... twenty seconds ... thirty seconds. Tracy studied the minute hand on the round white kitchen clock. Drip ... drip ... drip went the sink tap into the gleaming steel basin. She wanted to tighten it, but didn't dare. Her glance strayed to Auntie Nadia's pale, set face, shifted quickly back to the clock ... forty seconds ... fifty seconds ... and came to rest on Peter.

She had been in Ireland for five days, and her aunt and cousin had done nothing but fight.

'Clear the table,' Auntie Nadia repeated.

'I'm an Ulster warrior.' Peter stayed glued to his chair. 'Warrior heroes don't do women's work.'

Auntie Nadia's thin voice became thinner and tighter. She said, 'We're waiting for you to clear the table.'

Eighty seconds ... ninety seconds ... There really wasn't much to be cleared, Tracy thought. *Her* mum would never have made a heavy scene like this out of a few dirty plates and three place mats.

'Waahoo!' Peter's sudden ear-splitting whoop made her jump. 'I feel my battle fury coming on. Out of my way.' He charged backwards and forwards at a furious rate, slamming the plates on top of each other and banging them into the sink.

If Auntie Nadia was relieved, she didn't show it. Wearily she massaged the back of her neck with the tips of her fingers. 'Go to your room,' she said when he had finished.

'Waahoo!' whooped Peter. And went.

When all the dishes had been washed, dried and put away in Auntie Nadia's spotlessly neat kitchen cupboards, Auntie Nadia sat down in the painted rocking-chair beside the door and shut her eyes.

Tracy hated the thought of disturbing her, but the question was urgent, and there was nobody else she could ask. 'Excuse me, Auntie Nadia,' she said in a nervous squeak. 'How long would it take a letter to travel from here to Uganda?'

'About ten days,' Auntie Nadia murmured. 'You're going to write your parents? That's a good idea. You'll find a pad of airmail paper in the desk in your room.'

Auntie Nadia's house was a dormer bungalow built in the shape of a tissue box with a matchbox stuck on the side. Tracy had been given the attic room over the pinewood extension. Above the desk a small latticed window looked north towards the high grassy mound which Peter called Emain Macha—seat of King Conchobar, home of the Red Branch Knights of Ulster.

'That's history. Nobody uses the Gaelic name now. The proper name is Navan Fort,' Auntie Nadia had snapped. Tracy didn't care what they called it. 'Horrible Hump,' she whispered under her breath.

She could feel a hot pricking behind her eyes. She turned away from the Hump to study her calendar, the one she had carried all the way from home, by train and boat. The picture was of Balmoral Castle and underneath the first four days of August had been turned into diagonal crosses with a black felt-tip. Tracy swallowed bravely. Saturday was almost over. She could put a cross through day number five as well. But no sooner had she lifted the felt-tip, than hopeless tears plopped down onto the card. What was the use? Her mum had been wrong. Time wasn't flying past. It was crawling ... crawling like a half-dead snail ... and marking calendars wouldn't make the slightest difference.

She put the calendar back into the desk and took out the airmail note-pad. *Killylea Road, Armagh*, she wrote at the top of the first crisp, wafery page. Then she had to stop, because the tears were plopping so fast they had smudged the address. Even if she wrote to her mum and dad that very minute to tell them how unhappy she was, there would be ten more crosses on the calendar before they got the letter and another ten before she had a reply.

She had to face the Horrible Hump-like truth.

Nothing short of a miracle would get her home before the end of the month.

Tracy tore off the smudged sheet and pulled the pad towards her.

'Dear God,' she scrawled at the top of the page. 'I am writing to you because I need a miracle. My name is Tracy. I am ten years old and have been sent to stay with my aunt and cousin in Ireland.

'They are both mad.

'My cousin is a bully and a freak, and my aunt acts like she'd drop off the edge of the universe if she stepped outside the front door.

'In case you think I am making a fuss about

nothing, let me tell you what happened today—which is the same as what happened the last three days.

'I spent all morning and all afternoon hanging about the Horrible Hump. I had nothing to do and no one to talk to. First thing after breakfast, Peter said he was going to practise heroic skills and warrior feats (that is the mad way he talks) and Auntie Nadia told me to go with him. She said she was relying on me to see he didn't mix with the wrong sort and that I was to tell her what he did. She had her eyes shut, so she didn't see Peter standing in the hall. As soon as we got outside he twisted my arm like a cork-screw up my back and made me promise to keep my mouth shut.

'I had to promise, God. Peter is bigger than I am and older. He doesn't just mix with the wrong sort, he *is* the wrong sort—the mean, sneaky, bullying sort. But I daren't tell Auntie Nadia.

'As usual the Knights of the Red Branch (that's the name of Peter's gang) were waiting for us at the Horrible Hump. Before I tell you what happened, I'd better explain about the leaders. They call themselves Brian the Brave and Martin the Mighty. They are even older than Peter and every bit as mad. They roar around on black Yamaha motor-bikes and when they take off their crash helmets their mothers probably faint. It looks as if they have tipped pots of poster paint over their heads. They have dyed their hair three different colours. Dark brown, medium yellow and brilliant red.

'Peter told me this is because the gang's *real* leader

11

(a warrior called Cuchulainn, who died more than two thousand years ago!) had hair like that.

'When we got to the Hump this morning Brian the Brave pointed at me and said: "Haven't you gone back to Alba yet, Celt?" (Alba is their name for Scotland.)

'Peter said: "No chance! She's here for a month. But she knows the only way to keep healthy is to wear zips on her lips." Then he shoved me off the bank down into the ditch.

'I stayed in the ditch for three whole hours. I watched the gang practising their Apple feats, Salmon leaps and Heroes' screams. (This means juggling with apples, jumping over a rope and squealing like pigs.)

'Then I listened to their meeting. It was spooky. They made a circle round a yew tree and Peter recited something about Cuchulainn, their dead leader. (Peter is always reading things from a book he carries around everywhere with him.) The bit he recited was about Cuchulainn leaping into his chariot which was all covered in swords and knives and nails and axes, and charging round chopping the heads off his enemies.

'The Knights cheered so hard when he finished you'd have thought Cuchulainn had scored the winning goal in a football match.

'After that Martin the Mighty made an announcement. He said: "Weapon training this afternoon. Report to the headquarters at two o'clock sharp."

'Brian the Brave looked over at me and said: "What about her?"

'Peter made a scornful face and said: "No problem. She can stay in Emain Macha and get on with her embroidery."

'Peter is always saying mad and cruel things like that, God. Last year I knitted a scarf and a tea-cosy for my Brownies Make Things Challenge on the Brownie Road, but any normal person would know I couldn't get on with craft-work in a ditch. It was just something Peter read in his *Irish Tales and Legends* book that put the idea in his head. What he really meant was that I would have to spend another whole afternoon hanging around the Horrible Hump.

'There is nothing mouldier than hanging around a Hump hour after hour, hundreds of miles away from your family and friends. I know that now. Only two things happened all afternoon. First a group of Americans arrived. I could tell they were Americans because the men wore pink pants (that's what they call their trousers). They got out of their minibus and walked to the top of the Hump, studying the official notices on the way up.

'Then they left, and I felt lonelier than ever. I climbed up to the top of the Hump myself to see if there was any sign of Brian the Brave's motorbike with Peter on the back, but there wasn't. All I saw was hills and trees and fields and hedges and, on my left, a big empty quarry, and Auntie Nadia's house in the distance, with the blinds shut. And then the second thing happened. A landrover towing a bright yellow caravan pulled up outside a field about a quarter of a mile down the road. For a moment, when I saw that caravan, I felt hopeful. I thought perhaps a family had come to the Hump for their summer holidays. And I thought how great it would be if there was a girl my own age, and we could be friends and do things together. And then I remembered that Auntie Nadia was relying on me to stay with Peter and that Peter was ready to brain me if I opened my mouth. I didn't look at the caravan any more then, God. I didn't want to see any girls my own age, knowing I daren't go anywhere near them to say hello.

'Peter was in his usual bullying mood when he came back. He was bragging too. He bragged that he had done the ton on the back of Martin the Mighty's motorbike. Then he bragged that the Knights were working on a secret weapon. Once it was perfected, he said, it would be as dangerous as Cuchulainn's lightening spear which entered the body as one blade and burst into thirty barbs inside so that it couldn't be pulled out without bringing half the guts.

'I asked him who they were planning to use it on.

'"On the enemies of Ulster, of course," he said, with a scornful look. "And on Alban girls who tell tales."

'That made me feel worse than ever. It is very hard not to tell tales, God, because Auntie Nadia asks so many questions. I really believe the reason she invited me over was to have someone to spy on Peter.

'This evening I told her that we'd walked into Armagh and looked at letters and coins and stuffed animals in the museum.

'Now I am scared she'll find out it was a lie.

'I need a miracle, God. I really have to get out of here tomorrow or Monday at the latest. There is no way I can stick Auntie Nadia and Peter, the Knights and the Horrible Hump any longer. If you let me go home, I promise I will do anything you want. I will be really helpful and work hard at school. I will eat every kind of vegetable. I will never tell another lie. So please, if you care for me the tiniest bit, please, please do something fast. Yours sincerely, Tracy MacArthur. Amen.'

As Tracy signed her name to her letter, there was a knock on the door. Auntie Nadia poked her head in. She had tied her hair tightly back from her face, so her nose stuck out.

'Ah, I see you've finished your letter to your parents. Don't bother to seal the envelope. I was going to write myself, but there isn't much news. I'll just put a note on the end.'

'Oh no!' squeaked Tracy. 'You can't.' She felt her cheeks turn crimson. 'I mean, you can when I've written to them, but I haven't got round to their letter yet.'

Auntie Nadia said: 'I see,' in a flat voice. Her eyes were fixed on the closely-written sheets on the desk. 'You've been upstairs for a long time. Who have you been writing to?'

'A friend in Scotland,' Tracy gulped.

'Why use airmail paper to write to Scotland?'

'I don't have any other type. I haven't been writing to my parents, Auntie Nadia. Honest.'

Auntie Nadia didn't speak. Her gaze travelled to

the overnight bag beside the desk. Tracy flushed even redder. There was a folder inside with a packet of Care Bear notelets. But how could her aunt know about it? Had she X-ray eyes or something? With a sudden shiver, Tracy thought she understood why Auntie Nadia never went out. She had to stay in the house so she could fill every room with her strange, cold, knowing power; those dark shadowed eyes lighting on the least speck of dust, her thin hands constantly moving things, dusting under them, polishing, wiping out every corner and crack so that not the tiniest insect could creep into the house for shelter without being spotted. Helplessly the girl gathered up the airmail pages on her desk. She felt like an unusual beetle wriggling under a microscope. Auntie Nadia would keep peering until her observations were complete.

'Waahoo!' Peter burst upon the silence. He charged towards the window, chanting feverishly. 'Cuchulainn squeezed one eye narrower than the eye of a needle; he opened the other wider than a goblet. He bared his jaws to the ear; he peeled back his lips to the eye-teeth till his gullet showed.'

For the first time Tracy felt thankful her cousin was mad. He was leaning across the desk now, one eye half-shut, the other wide open, lips pulled back, teeth jutting out, pretending to be a warrior hero.

'We're being invaded,' he whooped. 'The enemy has set up camp on Red Branch land.'

'For a fourteen-year-old you are really very childish, Peter,' said Auntie Nadia.

'Childish!' Peter hammered his fist down on the

wooden top. 'This is a warrior's fist. The arm of a prodigy. Say that again and I'll smash the window.'

Auntie Nadia raised her eyebrows and shrugged.

'You'd better not. You'll only cut yourself,' said Tracy.

'Watch me bleed to death all over your letter, then,' whooped Peter, and to Tracy's horror he snatched the top page out of her grasp.

'Give me that! It's mine!' Desperately she grabbed the sheet and pulled. The paper tore. Peter was left with a flimsy strip in his hand.

'You're not to read it,' Tracy shrieked. 'It's a private letter. Auntie Nadia, tell him to give it back.'

'Give that to me, Peter,' said Auntie Nadia.

'No! No! It's mine!'

'Dear God,' read Peter, 'I am writing to you because I need a miracle .... Gosh!' He tossed the scrap onto the desk and grinned at his mother. 'No wonder she didn't want us to see it. She's up with the canaries!'

'You shouldn't speak about your cousin like that!' said Auntie Nadia faintly. 'Apologise.' Her face was so white, Tracy wondered if she was ill.

'But she's written to *God*. Remember what you said about people believing stuff like that. You said it was crazy.'

'What I believe is my business. And what Tracy believes is her business. Now, go to your room.'

Without another word Peter stumped out, shaking his head like a dog that had snapped at a fly and swallowed a wasp. He was confused. And angry.

He'll take this out on me tomorrow, thought Tracy fearfully.

Auntie Nadia, too, had turned to leave.

'Goodnight.' Her hand seemed to tremble on the door knob. Again Tracy thought she looked very pale. But her voice was back to normal: quiet, cold and firm. 'Go to bed now. We can write to your parents in the morning.'

Despite this instruction Tracy sat at the window for half an hour after her aunt had gone. It was almost dark. The sky above the mound had become a mottled mass of pink and rose-coloured blotches and the black silhouettes of the trees stood out against them—stark and jagged. Red Branch land. The title fitted. Dreamily Tracy studied the scene, hoping to find a message on the skyline—a comforting bump that would tell her the caravan she had seen that afternoon was still parked near the mound. No such shape presented itself. She did notice a small light gleaming in the quarry area, though. Had it been there before? She thought not—which meant it could well be the curtained glow from a caravan window.

She heard a click on the opposite side of the landing. Peter had switched off his bedside lamp. She was relieved. She would sleep better tonight. The rectangular glass panels beneath the lintels of both doors meant that any light in Peter's bedroom shone across into her own. Sometimes Peter's lamp shone right through till the morning and kept waking her up. She was sure her cousin didn't spend the whole night reading. Probably he just fell asleep with his tatty Cuchulainn book on his chest.

At home, when Tracy fell asleep like that, her mum would creep in, put the book back on the shelf and pull up the bedclothes.

Tracy could never imagine Auntie Nadia doing the same.

She *could* imagine her snooping round the bedroom, opening drawers, checking through the contents of wastepaper baskets before emptying them, to see what she could discover. It was as if a red light went on in Tracy's mind. She would have to be careful. She needed a hiding place for her letter; somewhere to store it for a day or two, safe from Auntie Nadia's prying eyes, until it could be safely tossed into a Scottish litter bin, worlds away from this house.

After a few minutes' consideration Tracy got up from the desk. She folded the tell-tale sheets of airmail paper into a tiny square and tucked them into the soap-box in her wash-bag.

She pulled on a night-shirt and climbed into bed. She thought: Auntie Nadia will never look there, and then she thought: the fifth day is over, and then she fell asleep.

CHAPTER TWO

What was going on? By this hour of the morning Auntie Nadia was usually swooping around with a duster, but today she was still in her dressing-gown, studying her reflection in the hall mirror. Tracy stood on the stairs and gaped.

'Ah, there you are, Tracy,' Auntie Nadia said. 'Wake Peter, and tell him to get ready quickly. We're going to church.'

Still wondering if she was seeing and hearing correctly, Tracy obeyed—more or less. Of course she didn't dare open Peter's bedroom door. She just battered on the outside as hard as she could, then scuttled back to the kitchen.

Ten seconds later Peter roared in: 'Do you know what Cuchulainn did to the screwball who woke him? He punched him on the forehead with his fist and drove the dome of his forehead back into his brain.'

Tracy wrapped her ankles round the legs of the stool and sat tight.

'And the same will happen to you, you little Alban toad, if you ever try that again.'

'Your mother sent me to tell you we're going to church,' she said primly.

Her cousin's mouth dropped open in amazement. 'Church! We haven't been there in years ... not since ...' He stopped and sat down suddenly, clenching his fists. 'You're making it up, aren't you, toad? She never said any such thing.'

Even as he spoke, there was the click of high heels on the parquet hall and Auntie Nadia appeared in the doorway. Tracy gasped and Peter stared.

Auntie Nadia said: 'I'm going to start the car engine. I'll see you outside in ten minutes.'

Peter kept staring. Then he muttered: 'You won't see me. I'm busy.'

'Doing what?' No amount of eye make-up could disguise the hungry, peering look in his mother's eyes.

He shifted uneasily. 'Nothing. I'll come if I have to, I suppose.'

Auntie Nadia nodded and clicked out.

Tracy watched the scene in a daze of admiration. It was the first time she had ever seen her aunt without an apron and slippers. How different she looked from the scraggy, colourless aunt of the last five days. This new Auntie Nadia wore rouge, coral lipstick and creamy gold eye-shadow. The skirt of her suit was a little too long, but the material shimmered when it caught the light. She had moved like a model—hat at an angle, braided head held high, long black clip-on ear-rings swinging as she turned.

'Ouch!' Tracy was brought back to her own misery by Peter kicking her viciously in the shin.

'This is all *your* fault,' he hissed. 'You put this

church idea into her head, you and your stupid letter last night. Now I have to miss the Red Branch meeting. Brian and Martin'll probably dissect you up when they hear about this.'

Tracy's leg still hurt when they left the house. Auntie Nadia had backed the car out of the garage. The bodywork gleamed as if it had just come through a car-wash. Inside, though, it smelled musty. 'The mats are damp. I'll air them tomorrow,' Auntie Nadia said, turning on the fan heater. Then she took a bottle of cologne from her handbag and sprayed its ferny smell around their feet.

The car spluttered out of the driveway.

'Too much clutch and not enough juice,' growled Peter from the back.

'I know what I'm doing,' his mother snapped. But Tracy wasn't convinced.

Fortunately, out on the open road her aunt's driving improved. She drove in silence, holding the speed at a steady thirty-five miles an hour, gripping the wheel so tightly her knuckles turned white. Peter, for once, was silent too.

With a stab of longing Tracy remembered going to church at home. Yesterday, from the top of the mound, she had seen the spires of two cathedrals rising among the hills beyond the quarry. Her church at home didn't have a spire. It was a plain, stone building with grey railings—brilliant for swinging on with her friends.

'This time next week, I'll be with them,' she told herself. 'The miracle *will* happen. It *must*.'

It took a good ten minutes to reach the city centre.

Auntie Nadia parked the car opposite a huge grassy park surrounded by trees.

Peter had got over his rage and was in a teasing mood. 'They used to fight cocks and bait bulls in there,' he observed, while his mother locked the door. 'These days it's just cricket and rugby. Pity, eh?' He jostled Tracy off the pavement, pointing to a huge gloomy building at the far end of the Mall. 'That's where you'll end up if you aren't careful. That's the women's jail.'

Auntie Nadia stiffened. 'It's been closed for years, as you perfectly well know.'

'They have other ones, though,' Peter hissed defiantly in Tracy's ear. 'They could put you in a cell and lock you up for ever, just like ...'

'Be quiet!' His mother's icy fury stopped him dead.

They arrived at the church. To Tracy's amazement, the minister raced right onto the front steps to greet them. He was a plump, elderly man with a booming voice that reminded Tracy of the minister at home and made her more homesick than ever. His church didn't have a spire either—just a porch and a couple of pillars.

'Nadia Richards,' he boomed, clasping Auntie Nadia's hand between both of his. 'What a joy to see you! And Peter. My, hasn't he grown!'

'This is my niece, Tracy.' Auntie Nadia managed a smile. 'Tracy, this is the Reverend Entwhistle.'

'I'm an old family friend, you know,' the Reverend Entwhistle boomed, patting Tracy heavily on the head. 'God bless you, my dear. Come in.'

24

There were pillars inside the church too. Tracy followed Auntie Nadia behind one into a side pew. A bad place to sit. She thought she heard children talking in the pews beneath the pulpit at the front, but without leaning out round the pillar, it was hard to be sure. To pass the time she counted heads: eleven men, eighteen women, twenty-four chrysanthemums and seven hats.

The organ played, she ran out of things to count and her leg ached where Peter had kicked her. It made her look at the heads again. What sort of people did they belong to? she wondered. There was a fair-haired lady in the choir who looked very kind. Tracy imagined rushing over to her after the service, crying: 'Don't make me go back with Auntie Nadia. I'm so unhappy and afraid. Please arrange for me to go home.'

And then it happened. The oddest thing that Tracy had ever seen in church. The door of the vestry, which was situated directly ten pews in front of her, opened, and, instead of the Reverend Entwhistle, a figure in baggy trousers walked out. Baggy trousers, a black bowler and a patchwork jacket.

'Hey, did you see that!' exclaimed Peter, as every head in the church looked up.

Tracy slipped out of her seat and round the pillar for a proper view.

Yes, there really was a clown sitting in the front pew under the pulpit. And, yes, there were other children with him. He had his arm round one of them, and the others were giggling and pointing at his bulging patchwork pocket. What were they pointing at? Goodness! Her eyes grew wide. The clown had brought a tiny curly-haired dog to church!

Pink with delight, Tracy returned to her seat. 'Please can I sit beside him,' she begged.

'Certainly not,' said Auntie Nadia coldly. 'This is a service of worship—not a circus.'

'Dear friends, we are gathered together to praise God!' boomed the Reverend Entwhistle. And the service began.

Tracy fidgeted her way through hymns and prayers and readings, edging as close as she could to the end of the pew, trying to crane round the pillar. She wanted to watch the clown singing. Then, to pass the time, she pretended his dog had escaped. She imagined it running up the steps of the pulpit and catching hold of the Reverend Entwhistle's ankle, stopping his prayer very suddenly—with an 'ouch' instead of 'amen'.

Even though she knew this hadn't happened, Tracy beamed. The Reverend Entwhistle beamed back. Well I never! thought Tracy, pleased and surprised. 'He likes having a clown in his church.'

She was more pleased than ever at his next words: 'Girls and boys,' he boomed. 'As you see we have a very special visitor with us this morning.' He peered down over the rim of his spectacles. 'His name is Carlo, and I'm going to ask him to come and tell you about his work.'

There was a ripple of excitement as the clown climbed into the pulpit. Tracy raced round the pillar just in time to see him take the little dog from his pocket and set it on the blue velvet cushion.

'Say hello to the boys and girls, Scruffy,' he said. And Scruffy, who looked like a cross between a Yorkshire terrier and a toy poodle, lifted his nose in the air and yapped.

Everyone laughed.

Scruffy stood up on his hind legs and licked the clown's ear.

'He thinks you're all very rude,' Carlo said solemnly, 'laughing like that and not saying hello back.'

'Hello, Scruffy,' the children chorused. Scruffy wagged his tail and sat down.

'Scruffy is just one of my dogs,' Carlo went on. 'I've got a few more back at the van. They all wanted to come and meet you this morning, but I couldn't fit three large mongrels into my pocket.'

'You could have brought them on leads,' cried an excited voice at the front.

'That's an idea! But I've a better one. Tomorrow, I'm putting a tent up beside my van—it's parked in a field near here—so you can come and visit me. The Rescue Circus meetings will start at three o'clock every afternoon for the next two weeks. Got that? Every afternoon at three o'clock. Let's hear it.'

'Every afternoon at three o'clock!' shouted Tracy along with all the rest.

'Great,' said Carlo. 'The Reverend Entwhistle has leaflets for your parents explaining the programme. Now, I've got one more thing to tell you before I sit down. Hands up anyone who thinks Scruffy is a clever dog.'

All over the church hands shot up.

'That's good,' said the clown with a click of his fingers. 'That makes you happy, doesn't it, Scruffy?'

Scruffy yapped once, then placed his front paws on the clown's shoulder and licked the clown's ear.

Carlo looked embarrassed. 'Well, that's very nice of you to say so.' He ruffled the terrier's fur. 'Boys and girls, do you know what Scruffy told me just then? He said the reason he's so clever is because he believes I know best.' He nodded thoughtfully. 'And you know Scruffy has just reminded me of something in the Bible. The Bible tells me that a clever person is someone who believes God knows best. That's a very important lesson, isn't it? We're going to talk more about it in the meetings next week. But in the meantime, remember: a clever person is someone who believes God knows best. Will you remember that, girls and boys?'

'Yes,' Tracy yelled, and somehow her yell seemed louder and clearer than all the rest. The clown looked down at her and smiled.

'Shut up, toad.' Peter hauled her back to her seat. 'You're making a public show of us.'

When the service was over, the Reverend Entwhistle stood in the front porch with Carlo beside him, ready to shake hands with the congregation as they left.

Auntie Nadia had shot out of the pew the very minute the organ started, so she, Tracy and Peter were the first in the queue.

'Nadia, my dear,' the Reverend Entwhistle seemed unwilling to let go of her hand. 'Won't you stay and have a cup of coffee with us?'

'No,' said Auntie Nadia. 'No. Really. I couldn't.'

At this the Reverend Entwhistle had to release her because everyone else was being held up.

But Tracy caught hold of the clown's jacket. It was her only chance and she knew it. 'Please, Carlo.' She tugged at his arm. 'Please will you ask Auntie Nadia if I can come to your circus?'

'Is your aunt the lovely lady at the bottom of the steps?'

If Tracy had had longer she would have explained that Auntie Nadia usually looked like something washed up on the beach, but every second was taking her shimmering figure further from the church. 'Yes,' she nodded. 'Oh, hurry, please.'

'Right.' Carlo bounded down the steps, waving a bundle of yellow leaflets. 'Excuse me, madam. I've some information here about the Rescue Circus. Your niece would like to come, I believe.'

Auntie Nadia stopped and turned round. To Tracy's relief, she took a leaflet.

'You'll find the tent in a field near Navan Fort. Do you know where that is?'

'We live practically on top of it.'

Tracy was so excited now, she was hopping up and down. 'I saw you arrive yesterday. You have a bright yellow van.'

'That's right.' The clown winked. 'Amazing the way I got permission to park there—but that's another story.'

'Will you let me go, Auntie Nadia?' Though it would have taken a heart of stone to resist the pleading in Tracy's eyes, Auntie Nadia's heart was made of pretty tough material.

'We'll see,' she said coldly. 'One afternoon, perhaps, with Peter.'

'With Peter!' The girl tried to hide her dismay. 'But he'd be too old.'

'Nobody's too old for the Rescue Circus,' said the clown, with a grin in Peter's direction. 'The lad's as welcome as the flowers in May.'

Oh dear! Tracy saw trouble written all over her cousin's face. He was pretending to be Cuchulainn again: screwing up one eye, glaring with the other, pulling back his lips so that his teeth stuck out.

From inside Carlo's pocket Scruffy wriggled and barked.

'You've parked on Red Branch land,' Peter snarled. 'Don't talk to me about permission. You've no right to be there. No right, do you hear!'

He looked so strange that the children from the front row, who had followed the clown out of the church, huddled together and the smallest one started to cry.

Auntie Nadia turned on her heel and walked away—head high, back straight. Click click clickity clickity click click.

'Come and talk to me about it.' The clown gripped Peter's shoulder. 'Come before the meeting, or after the others have gone. Then we can have a proper chat.'

'Proper chat, my warp-spasm!' hissed Peter, shaking himself free. 'You just get off our land.'

'Don't mind him. Big problem in that home.

There! There!' The wailing child's mother comforted her toddler and whispered to the clown in one breath. Tracy overheard. Her cousin heard too. He turned on the woman as if about to devour her. Next minute, he had gone.

If it hadn't been for the clown Tracy would have told everything. She would have cried out that Auntie Nadia was cruel and Peter was mad and begged the woman to help her get back to Scotland. But the clown was standing beside her. 'See you tomorrow?' He raised one bushy eyebrow.

Tracy swallowed. She knew what he meant. He was asking her to be brave. To hang on. Long enough to visit the Rescue Circus. Another twenty-four hours. Could she? Dare she?

She didn't trust herself to speak. She simply gulped and nodded, then ran after Peter and Auntie Nadia down the street.

CHAPTER THREE

It was a long, lonely afternoon. Tracy sat in her bedroom, counting. She counted the beams in the roof (eight) and the diamond shapes on the lino (fifty-seven) and the number of times her heart beat every minute (seventy-four). When there was nothing in the room left to count, she turned her attention to the leaves on the cherry tree in the garden. 'Bother the wind. This is impossible!' She gave up after leaf 319 was unexpectedly grounded. For another seventy-four heart-beats she gazed hopelessly yet longingly towards the Rescue Circus, then, with a sigh, she picked up her pen.

'Dear God,' she wrote. 'As you see I am still here. This morning in church the clown told us a clever person is someone who believes you know best (he asked us to remember, and I have). When a person needs a miracle and doesn't get one, and they find themselves stuck in a place they don't want to be, are they still expected to be clever? It is very hard, God—you must admit.

'It is easier to believe you aren't there.

'That's what Auntie Nadia believes (Peter said so last night). The Reverend Entwhistle disagrees,

33

and so does the clown, and so do I. Most of the time.

'I believed you were there in church this morning, and I still believed it after church when I was standing beside the clown.

'Then I came back to Auntie Nadia's house and now I'm not so sure.

'This place is getting me down more than ever. Peter has gone to a Council of War and Auntie Nadia is in bed with a migraine. The only thing that stops me crying is the fact that I can see the clown's caravan through the bedroom window. Also I have a few questions. Some about you, some about the clown and some about Auntie Nadia.

'I will ask the questions about you first: Are you there? Do you really know best? Why haven't you done what I wanted?

'Now my questions about the clown: What is the inside of his caravan like? What are his other three dogs like? What will happen at his meetings?

'Before I ask about Auntie Nadia, I will tell you what happened when we got home.

'Auntie Nadia and Peter had a fight. It was the biggest fight they've had in the last six days, and I sat through it like a pea in a fruit salad feeling awful.

'The fight started the minute Auntie Nadia served out the dinner. (It would probably have started sooner, only Auntie Nadia didn't speak till then.) Auntie Nadia said: "You made a fool of yourself after church this morning, Peter."

'Peter waved his knife in the air and said: "The heavens are over us, the earth is beneath us, the seas

34

encircle us and unless the heavens with all their stars fall upon us or the earth gives way beneath us, or the seas flood in to drown the land, the Knights of the Red Branch will triumph over the enemy."

'"I've had enough of this nonsense." Auntie Nadia snatched his Cuchulainn book from his knee (he had been reading it while we waited for the potatoes), tore it in half and threw it in among the peelings in the pedal-bin.

'I thought Peter was going to hit her. But Auntie Nadia stopped him with one of her looks.

'She said, "If only you could see yourself, Peter. You're no Ulster hero. You're just a silly schoolboy with a head full of talk. People laugh at you behind your back."

'That made Peter feel small. I could tell by the way he went red. "No they don't," he muttered. "I heard them. They say I've a big problem at home."

'Then Auntie Nadia sort of crumpled over her dinner. (We still hadn't started eating and mine was getting cold.) She said: "People should mind their own business." She cut a piece of meat and stared into space. A few minutes later she said she had a migraine and would have to lie down.

'The moment she'd gone, Peter fished his Cuchulainn book out of the pedal-bin and stuck it back together with sellotape.

'I said, "Isn't it smelly?"

'He said, "Who cares? They didn't go in for washing in those days."

'Then he sat down and ate his dinner, and when his plate was empty, he started on Auntie Nadia's.

'I said, "What is your mum going to eat?"'

'He said, "Nothing. She won't be down till five o'clock. And anyway, I need strength for the Council of War."'

'Then he helped himself to more potato (he'd already had four) and told me that Cuchulainn could eat a whole buffalo in one go and drink a whole vat of wine, and that he would be able to do the same if he got a chance.'

'I said, "What's the Council of War about?" and he pinched me and said, "Nothing Alban girls need to hear."'

'He ate practically all the trifle before going out. I was left with the dishes.'

'So what do you think of that, God? Not very nice, was it?'

'Now for my question about Auntie Nadia: Do you think she has a skeleton in the cupboard? (I don't mean a real skeleton—although it might be.) I am suspicious. Why is she avoiding people? What is the big family problem the lady talked about? I am beginning to wonder if Uncle Joe died in an accident the way Mum said he did. (She didn't say he died, she just said he'd gone away, but I knew what she meant. She'd said the same about Honey, my hamster. And then the neighbour's dog dug him up.) Perhaps Auntie Nadia murdered him. That would explain why she got so angry when Peter mentioned the women's jail. The main thing is, I am sure she is hiding something.'

'But I don't want to stay here long enough to find out what.'

'God, I am trying to believe you are there, and I am trying to believe you know best, so now I am asking you to do two little things for me: (1) Please let me go to the Rescue Circus tomorrow. (2) Please let me go home the day after.

'Yours sincerely, Tracy MacArthur. Amen'

It was a quarter to five by the time she had finished her letter. Peter still had not returned. Tracy folded the pages and put them into her soap-box. Then she looked out of the window, feeling worried. Auntie Nadia would be mad if she came down and discovered that Peter had gone off on his own when they were meant to stay together.

'What'll I do if he isn't back by five?' she whispered, gazing at the yellow caravan for inspiration.

Suddenly she had an idea. It was almost as if the clown had put the thought in her head. Yes, she would risk it. After all, even if Auntie Nadia did have a guilty secret, she still hadn't eaten since breakfast.

Determined, yet at the same time marvelling at her daring, Tracy slipped down to the kitchen. She switched on the kettle. At five o'clock she was carrying a perfectly set tray complete with paper napkin, bunch of daisies in egg-cup, roast beef sandwiches and tea made with real tea-leaves towards Auntie Nadia's room. Her hands shook so much that the tea-cup rattled on its saucer. But she didn't turn back. Gently yet firmly she knocked on the bedroom door.

'It's Tracy. I've brought you a cup of tea. May I come in?' she called.

Even though there was no answer, she opened the door. She stepped into a darkened room faintly scented with flowers, set the tray down carefully on the bedside table and pulled the blind half-open. A shaft of light fell across the bed where her aunt lay, making the ivory sheets glisten. Auntie Nadia's face too was pearly white. With her dark hair spread across the pillow she looked, Tracy thought, like Sleeping Beauty on a bed of rose-petals—carved in ice.

'I've brought you a cup of tea,' she said again softly.

This time Auntie Nadia opened her eyes. But the fairy-tale feeling continued.

'What time is it, Margie?' she smiled drowsily.

Tracy understood. People were always saying she looked like her mum.

'I'm not Margery. I'm Tracy. I learned to make tea in Brownies, and I've brought you some.'

Even this matter-of-fact explanation had not broken the spell. Auntie Nadia's eyes became clearer, but her face did not harden.

'I was dreaming of the way things were when your mother and I were small,' she sighed.

The next half an hour was quite amazing. Auntie Nadia sat up in bed to drink her tea, and as she drank, she talked to Tracy about the past: about the games she and Margie had played together, about the parties they had gone to, about the secret hide-out they had built at the bottom of the garden.

'We took the first part of her name and the second part of mine; Mardia's Place, we called it. Margie

38

used to wake me early in the morning, before anyone else was up, and we would sneak down to it in our dressing-gowns and share a picnic breakfast with the birds.'

'Mum still gets up early,' Tracy observed.

'Yes. She was always the one who organised things. She was the adventurous one too.'

'She still is,' said Tracy. 'That's why she helps with missionary clinics in the holidays instead of sun-bathing in Marjorca. She isn't afraid of snakes or anything.'

Auntie Nadia had laughed at this—though a little sadly, Tracy thought. She seemed to be wishing herself back into the past. Suddenly she leaned over, opened a drawer in the bedside table and took out a tiny key.

'I've a suitcase full of photograph albums under the bed,' she said. 'We can look through them if you like.'

So they did. Tracy sat by her aunt's side on the bed, turning over page after page of photographs, and as she turned she saw Auntie Nadia growing from a chubby-cheeked bald-headed baby, into a pretty little girl in smocked dresses, and on into a long-haired teenager in a very short skirt.

'I've changed so much,' she murmured.

Tracy considered: 'You're thinner now, and you dress differently, but I'd still know who you were.' She did not add that the biggest difference was one of expression. The teenager was smiling—something Auntie Nadia almost never did.

'I trusted people then,' Auntie Nadia continued,

39

more to herself than anyone else, which was a relief, because Tracy couldn't think how to reply. The words reminded her that *she* didn't trust her aunt. In the silence that followed, she gazed round at the gold and ivory bedroom units, looking for clues—a bloodstain maybe, or a stray bone poking from a wardrobe—that would tell her what had happened to Uncle Joe.

'Have you some more recent photos—of your wedding perhaps?' she chanced.

The question jerked Auntie Nadia back to the present. 'No. I threw them all out,' she said, with a return to her old sharp tone.

Time was up. Tracy could see that the effect of the tea and sandwiches had worn thin. It was now or never if she was going to claim her reward. She hopped off the bed and lifted the tray, then turned boldly in the doorway, aiming to look and sound as much like her mother as possible.

'Please may I go to the Rescue Circus tomorrow? It would be such an adventure!'

'Very well.' Auntie Nadia leaned back, sighing, against her ivory pillows. 'There's just one condition: Peter will have to go too.'

CHAPTER FOUR

The sun, Tracy's teacher had said, was ninety-three million miles away from the earth. It hung in the sky, as Tracy could see for herself, like a brilliant, blazing dome. It did not, as far as Tracy knew, have an opening down its middle, but if it had had one, and if she had been able to travel across ninety-three million miles of space to slip inside, then she knew she would feel exactly the way she felt now, sitting in the clown's tent.

She had escaped to another world. Beneath her was a hard wooden bench, on either side were other children, chattering excitedly, before her was the round open space into which, she knew, the clown and his dogs would appear, and all around her—so limpid that she almost felt she could spread her arms and swim through it—was the golden glow of sunlight, diffused through yellow canvas.

Almost as important: the world she had left behind had taken a turn for the better. Of course Peter was as mad as ever, but yesterday evening they had done a deal. A warrior's pledge, he called it. She had handed over the five pound note her dad had slipped into her hand just before she got onto the boat, and he had agreed to pretend to go with her to the Enemy Stronghold (his name for the clown's tent). That way she could do what she wanted, and he could do what he wanted, and Auntie Nadia would be none the wiser. Tracy had been surprised and delighted to find him so co-operative. The money was only a loan, after all. What's more he had given her something for the clown. A message in a grubby brown envelope. An apology, to judge from the embarrassed way he had handed it over, without looking her straight in the face—as if he was ashamed of himself. For a minute Tracy had nearly liked him. She had been grateful to him, not just for doing a deal, but for giving her this opportunity to speak to the clown. But then he had spoiled it, shrugging off her thanks and muttering that she was nothing but a female pawn of the Enemy and the sooner she went back to Alba the better.

Ta tatara tatarum. A fanfare of trumpets snatched her thoughts back to the ring. Any minute now! She wriggled her toes in excitement, noting the table covered in a fringed velveteen cloth which had been wheeled into the centre. What would it be used for? She was glad she was still here. She was glad she had stayed long enough to find out what the Rescue Circus was about.

The background music grew louder ... and louder. *Ta tatara tatara tatarum.* The clown burst in. Hands ... feet ... hands ... feet ... he cartwheeled heavily from the entrance to the curtained table, followed, like the Pied Piper of Hamlin, by a tumbling jumble of legs and tails.

One final turn and he was upright, his arms stretched out wide, as if he wanted to hug the whole audience. 'Hello everybody,' he called while the legs and tails unjumbled themselves into four separate dogs—one enormous, two medium-sized and Scruffy.

Tracy felt a lump rise in her throat. She was so pleased to see him again—broader, brighter and kinder than ever. Today, in place of the patchwork jacket (his Sunday best?) he wore a full-sleeved white shirt under a fluorescent yellow bib. His name—CARLO—was printed in big black letters on the front, and the words RESCUE CIRCUS were printed on the back.

'Hello, Carlo,' she cried with all the rest.

The next hour seemed to be gone in a couple of minutes.

First the clown introduced them to his dogs: huge, gangly Goliath, silky golden Sheba, solemn-eyed Ears, and Scruffy—the clown's favourite, Tracy suspected, because he was so small and mischievous. The other three dogs had all been able to do something clever. Sheba could catch balls, Ears could jump through hoops and Goliath had made everyone laugh by rolling onto his back and waggling his legs in the air. All Scruffy had done was steal the orange handkerchief hanging out of Carlo's pocket and scuttle off with it under the table. But afterwards, Tracy noticed, he got a pat on the head and a dog biscuit just like the others.

And Carlo had picked him up and held him under one arm while he taught them the Rescue Circus song. He had begun with a very straight face, telling them how important and meaningful a song it was. Then, from behind the tablecloth, he had produced a crazy jingle, printed out in black on a bright yellow sheet.

Wag wag woofle whine
Widdle whack ho!

The words had sounded crazier than ever the way he sang them, getting everyone, even the six rude boys at the back, to join in—slowly at first, then faster and faster and higher and higher until the craziest moment of all, when Goliath had pointed his shaggy wolf-head to the roof of the tent and howled.

Afterwards, though, there had been a problem.

The boys at the back kept singing when everyone else had stopped. Tracy had turned round and glared at them. If she had been in charge of the Rescue Circus, she would have had them thrown out, but the clown just carried on as if nothing was wrong, explaining in his powerful, easy-going voice that his dogs always liked to award a prize to the boy or girl in the audience with the juiciest pair of feet.

'Now then,' a smile had broken out all over his weatherbeaten face, 'I've learned something important. I've learned that kids with extra juice in their feet get extra restless—which means I can always tell where the juicy feet are in my audiences, because their owners always create a lot of noise.'

Grinning more broadly than ever he had gestured towards the back row.

'So that's where our juicy feet are today, folks. Up there. In the back row. OK, lads. Down you come.'

Abruptly the singing stopped.

'This is your big chance,' the clown continued, pulling a stool, a basin and sponges from under the table. 'One of you will leave this tent with the Foot of the Week Award. Just let me get set up here! That's it! We're ready for you now.'

Whistling, hooting and shoving, the six trooped into the ring.

Their ringleader, a stocky, snub-nosed lad called Jimbo, pulled off his Doc Martens as Carlo explained the rules: competitors were to remove their right sock and boot, sit down on the stool and stick their bare foot into Goliath's wicker basket. The dog would sniff it then, according to its juiciness, award a number of licks.

Jimbo, meanwhile, had hitched up his denims to display a garish pair of red, white and blue striped socks. 'Me granny knit them,' he yelled at the cheering audience. 'Ready when you are, dawg.' He peeled the right one off and tossed it across the ring.

'One last condition.' The clown wrapped an arm round his shoulder. 'Goliath expects all feet to be washed before he sniffs them.'

To even louder cheers from the audience, he handed each competitor a sponge.

It didn't take Tracy long to work out that one of those sponges had been filled with marrowbone jelly. Why else would Goliath have slobbered all over Jimbo's foot?

'Gerroff! Yer dawg's nose is cauld, mister. An' 'is

tongue feels like slime,' the winner of the award had shrieked in delight.

Thoughtfully, she fingered the envelope in her pocket. She felt a faint twinge of regret that she hadn't tried a bit harder to persuade Peter to come with her. Of course she knew her cousin was awful. But Jimbo had been awful too (though in a more normal way)—and look at the effect the clown had had on him! He was in the front row now, displaying his award (a huge, pink, hairy cardboard foot), rocking back on his chair, grinning round at his friends—but listening, yes definitely listening to every word.

They had reached the serious part of the programme.

Carlo had heaved himself onto the table. Scruffy was curled up at his side. Goliath, Sheba and Ears had piled round his feet. Suddenly, after all the noise and laughter, the tent seemed amazingly peaceful and quiet.

It was the expression in his sea-blue eyes that had spread this calm; the way he sat looking unhurriedly from face to face. He had recognised her, Tracy knew. For a split second those eyes had rested on her face and she had felt gladness, like a laser beam, pouring from them.

And finally he began to talk.

'There are times,' he said, 'when people let you down. Friends let you down. Even family let you down. And you let them down too. Right?'

He paused. The tent was so still Tracy thought she could hear Goliath snore. Suddenly a horrible thought struck her. What if Peter let her down? What if he didn't keep his side of the bargain? They wouldn't arrive home together then. Auntie Nadia would discover she had been tricked.

'People are always letting other people down,' the clown continued. 'Animals too. They get let down. Take Scruffy here, for example,' he ruffled the little dog's fur. 'When I found him three years ago, his back was covered in sores. He hadn't had anything to eat for days, and he was so frightened I could hardly get near him. Someone—some family, or even some boy or girl your own age, had let him down badly. Bought him, then decided they didn't want him. Didn't bother trying to find him another home, just kicked him out on the side of the road.'

For the second time Tracy felt a lump in her throat; only this time it was a lump of sadness. She wasn't quite sure whether thinking about Scruffy or about Auntie Nadia had put it there. Once Scruffy had trusted his owner ... just like Auntie Nadia had trusted her. Oh dear! Why did things have to be so complicated? Had she been wrong to lend Peter the money?

The next part of the clown's story really made her think. He told them that Goliath, Sheba and Ears had been let down too. Goliath had been starved, Sheba chained up in a cold dark shed, while Ears was left to wander the streets.

'I found him cowering behind a dustbin. If the dog warden had got to him first—well, the chances are, he wouldn't be around today. In fact the chances are that none of these dogs would be around today—if they hadn't been ...'

'Rescued,' Tracy shouted before she could stop herself.

The clown raised his bushy eyebrows and smiled.

'Please,' she continued, the words tumbling out almost tearfully over the lump. 'I know how your circus got its name. It's because all your dogs were rescued after being let down.'

'Absolutely right,' said the clown. 'The dogs you see here have all been rescued. And what's more—their owner's been rescued too. There was a time, years ago, when he thought everyone had let him down; when he felt angrier than Goliath, lonelier than Sheba and more confused than Ears. And then he found someone to help him; someone he could really trust; not a human friend, this time, but someone who knew exactly what being human was like. Tomorrow I'll tell you more about it, but for today the thing I want you to remember is this: God is a wonderful Rescuer and he never lets anyone down. Have you got that?'

'God is a wonderful Rescuer and he never lets anyone down,' Tracy repeated thoughtfully. 'God is a wonderful Rescuer and he ... hey, that's brilliant.' Suddenly, the lump was gone. She had forgotten all her worries. She felt so happy that if she had still had her fiver, she would have bought a huge bag of sweets and passed it round the whole audience, including Jimbo—even though he had started making rude signs. She knew now that she would *definitely* be going home tomorrow. God couldn't let her down.

Not after what the clown had said. He would deal with request number two as favourably as he had dealt with number one. There would be a letter waiting for her back at the house; or a telephone message perhaps. Auntie Nadia would explain the situation coldly and calmly. 'I'm sorry, Tracy, but your parents have altered their plans. They have discovered that there are more than enough doctors and water engineers in Uganda already, so they are flying back home. You will return by boat tomorrow and meet them at Glasgow Airport.'

Of course it wouldn't be polite to cheer. For her aunt's sake, Tracy knew, she must try to look surprised, even a little disappointed at the news. And when she thought of it, there *was* a disappointing side to her miracle.

'Goodbye. See you tomorrow,' Carlo was calling.

'See you tomorrow,' she heard everyone else reply.

She had not been able to join in. She was sorry about that; sorry to miss the rest of the meetings; sorry, also, to lose her fiver. (She couldn't imagine Peter being heroic enough to return the money by post.)

But at least she had the envelope he had given her.

With a sense of importance, Tracy moved out of her seat. She had been looking forward to this moment. And now it seemed more special than ever. Her last opportunity to speak to the clown, to explain what had happened, to pat Scruffy on the head one last time and say goodbye.

'Remember me?' Five minutes of ducking and squeezing had brought her to the centre of the ring where he stood. 'I'm Tracy.'

'Tracy!' He clasped her shoulder, and there was no doubting the warmth of the welcome which beamed from his sea-blue eyes. 'So Auntie said "yes".'

'Sort of.' She hesitated.

'Sort of?'

'Well, I was meant to bring Peter, but he wouldn't come. He asked me to give you this.'

The envelope looked grimier than ever when she produced it.

'Well, well.' The clown released her shoulder to break the seal.

'He wanted to say sorry,' said Tracy. No sooner were the words out of her mouth than she realised how very unlike Peter they sounded. Her heart sank. Oh no! What *had* he said?

Deftly, with large, blunt fingers, the clown unfolded the printed sheet. His smile faded. Tracy peered at it over his elbow, then turned away, biting her lip.

She ought to have known. She ought to have known it wouldn't be an apology.

But how could she ever have known it would be something as horrible as this? Of course she remembered the picture. She had seen it in his Cuchulainn book—that illustration of his dead hero's amazing boyhood strength. It had seemed hateful then, but it was one hundred times more hateful now, torn out and hanging limply between the clown's finger and thumb. Peter's message. No apology—just a stupid, mad, horrible threat.

The picture of a huge hopeless dog being cudgelled to death.

CHAPTER FIVE

Nothing shocked the clown. He just seemed to absorb cruelty like a mop and squeeze out kindness. 'Peter needs help,' he said. Not, 'Peter needs to be strung upside down by his toes till he sees what a mean rotten bully he is.'

Of course Tracy wasn't quite sure whether Carlo fully understood what her cousin was like. 'Talk to him,' he said. 'Tell him what happens at the Rescue Circus. Tell him he can bring his friends if he wants.'

But how did you talk to someone who would probably twist your wrist and screw it up your back as soon as you opened your mouth?

They had discussed this problem, along with a number of other things—including the question of when Tracy would return home—over a glass of orange juice on the caravan steps. Half-way through this discussion, Jimbo, who had been helping to sweep the tent, plonked himself on the steps beside them.

To Tracy's surprise, he'd proved a lot more sensible than he looked. He'd known all about the Knights of the Red Branch. A crowd of spacers, he called them, but he still thought their threat should be taken seriously. 'Nobody minds a bit of messin', but that Martin and Brian—they're up to no good. Been in trouble with the police, they have.'

He'd even managed to come up with a suggestion. His idea was that they should tell Peter about something he'd seen in the *Armagh Gazette*—an article outlining the planned development scheme for the land around Navan Fort.

'They're going to turn this whole place into a leisure park with a shop and a cafe and exhibitions and archeologists and tickets and all. So what's the point of throwing a wobbler over a tent and one wee caravan?'

'Right,' the clown had nodded. 'If he could just stop classing me as the enemy. Then perhaps we could get at the real problem.'

If Tracy had had longer she would have asked what he thought the *real* problem was, but it was already ten minutes to five and she had arranged to meet her cousin at the bottom of the Hump at five o'clock. That way they would keep Auntie Nadia thinking they had been together by returning home at the same time.

'I have to go now,' she said as she reluctantly rose to her feet. For a long moment she looked round at the tent and the caravan and the dogs, storing every detail in her memory. Then in one quick movement she thrust her glass into the clown's hand and turned on her heel. 'Thanks for the orange. Goodbye.'

'Hey, hang on a minute! I'm coming with you,'

called Jimbo. 'The sooner I speak to yer cousin about that piece in the paper the better. Right?'

The smell of sizzling bacon drifted across the road. Carlo had his supper on the stove. Wisps of smoke floated out of his caravan chimney, while outside all his dogs, except Scruffy (who was probably inside waiting for titbits) lay stretched out on the grass enjoying the late afternoon sun.

Tracy and Jimbo leaned side by side against the railings.

'I'd love to live in a caravan,' Tracy said.

Jimbo sighed. 'I'd sell me socks for a bacon buttie.'

'Wouldn't that hurt your granny's feelings?'

'Aw, she wouldn't care. She's gone and emigrated to America.'

Tracy giggled. She could just picture Jimbo's granny outside her ranch in a rocking-chair, knitting socks with stars and stripes. As for Jimbo, she liked him. Of course he was a dreadful show off. Even while they waited, he kept turning round to wave his cardboard foot at a family picnicking under the beech trees at the edge of the mound. But he didn't mean any harm and he really seemed keen to help Peter.

If only Peter would hurry. Her former anxiety returned. What if he didn't show up?

'Come on, Jimbo,' she tugged her waving companion's faded sleeve. 'Let's walk up the lane to the quarry and wait for him there.'

A quarter of an hour later they were still leaning against the quarry gate, overlooking disused corrugated sheds and piles of rubble. 'Yeah, well, he never was much of a time-keeper,' Jimbo remarked. 'He had a great line in excuses, though. I mind one time he taul our form teacher he'd been resuscitatin' a frog.'

Tracy's mouth dropped. Until that moment she had thought that Jimbo and her cousin were strangers. 'You mean you're in the same class at school?'

'Used to be.' Jimbo kicked a stone with the side of his boot and sent it flying over the gate. 'Until his aul man ... well ... you know.'

'Died?'

Now it was Jimbo's turn to look astonished. 'Copped it, you mean? Naw. Who told you that?'

'My mother,' said Tracy, more confused than ever.

'Ah well ...' Jimbo seemed to be struggling for words. 'If that's what she said, then that's the way it is. I mean your ma would know best, wouldn't she? Being a relative and that.'

Tracy looked him full in the face. 'That's a load of bananas.' She continued plaintively, 'I can't get anyone to tell me the truth about Uncle Joe. Please, Jimbo. Please tell me what happened.'

He stared back, reddening, then hurriedly glanced at his watch. 'Flip! Would you look at the time! I gotta go. Me granny'll murder me if I'm not back before six.' He picked up his cardboard foot. 'See you tomorrow.'

'I won't be here,' muttered Tracy.

'And your granny's in America,' she yelled at his departing back.

Left. Right. Left. Right. Up the path. Wait on the doorstep. Turn the handle. Open the door. Stand in the hallway.

Issuing firm instructions to her legs to stop them from running in the opposite direction, Tracy slipped into the house.

There was no sign of Peter. No thumping, banging or whooping to indicate that he had come home first. Auntie Nadia, she reckoned, must be lying back on the chair in the kitchen—pale, tense, and opening her eyes at regular intervals, with growing irritation, to check the clock.

Tracy had two hopes in the situation, and both depended on her reaching her room undetected. First and most importantly she hoped (no, she was *certain*) that she would find her miracle letter on her desk. And secondly she hoped to hide from Auntie Nadia, like a mouse in a hole, only popping out when Peter arrived.

Clutching the handrail and placing her feet with care, she crept up the narrow wooden stairway. So far, so good. There had been the odd creak, but no cold flat voice from the kitchen calling, 'Tracy, is that you?'

A dozen stealthy steps carried her to her bedroom door. It was open. Funny, she thought, I didn't leave it that way.

'Ahhh!'

In the seconds that followed she wasn't sure from whose mouth the sound came. Maybe both she and Auntie Nadia had screamed together. There was no doubt about it—they had given each other a terrible shock.

'T-Tracy!' Auntie Nadia spoke first, in short gasps, leaning back against the window-sill. 'I didn't hear you come in. I was just ... er ... looking for something. The ten pound note I'd set aside to pay the milkman, actually ... I thought I'd dropped it here ... But of course it probably isn't lost at all.... Probably I've just put it in an extra safe place and forgotten ... somewhere I'd never think of like ... like....' she gestured helplessly.

'A soap-box.'

'Well ... yes.'

They stared at each other warily.

Then came the question Tracy had been dreading. Her aunt's awkwardness stiffened into a peer of suspicion. 'But where's Peter?'

'He's ... he's ... still at the Rescue Circus,' Tracy stammered, 'helping the clown to sweep the tent. He sent me on to explain so that you wouldn't worry about us being late for tea.'

Auntie Nadia nodded at this and even managed a faint smile. 'You must think I'm very fussy,' she said, in the same confiding voice she had used in the bedroom the previous day. 'I can't seem to stop worrying about Peter. Things have been so difficult these last couple of years. He's a good boy at heart, but he ... he acts so strangely at times. I couldn't bear it if he got into trouble. I really couldn't, you know.'

'I know,' said Tracy.

'Well, I'd better get downstairs and check the oven. I do hope Peter won't be long.' She moved away from the window, unblocking Tracy's view of the desk.

The girl's heart descended into her track shoes. It was bad enough having to tell lies about Peter, but what she saw now made her misery complete.

The top of the desk was as bare as a winter branch.

There had been no miracle.

As Auntie Nadia padded down the stairs (she was wearing her slippers and apron once more), Tracy stared emptily from the window to the desk and back to the window again. And gradually in place of the emptiness she felt anger. It was all very well for the clown to warn her this might happen. It was all very well for him to wonder whether God wanted her to stay a while longer. He didn't have to live in this dreary house. He had his cosy caravan, with his own fridge and his gas stove and his tape deck and his TV, all bright and cheerful with just the right amount of mess. *And* he didn't have any relatives. Or if he did, they weren't the sort who made your life a funeral. Oh yes, it was easy for him to talk about God knowing best and never letting anyone down. She disagreed. Totally. If God intended to keep her here, then in her opinion he was making his biggest mistake since wasps.

The girl sighed. She still felt as empty and angry and argumentative as ever, but there wasn't much point in arguing with the clown—especially when he wasn't there. He had only warned her, after all. He wasn't the one who had turned down her request.

Grimly she opened the desk and took out her pad of airmail paper.

'Dear God,' she scrawled, and then crossed out the

dear. 'This will probably be my last letter. I wouldn't be writing at all except I want you to know how badly you have let me down.

'Here I am, waiting to be rescued, and what do you do? Nothing.

'What's worse, you break your promises. You let me go to the Rescue Circus and listen to the clown and build up my hopes. Only to dash them to pieces.

'You will be pleased to know that your friend, the clown, did his best to prepare me for this. He said that sometimes you rescue people by taking them out of difficult situations, but sometimes you give them special help instead.

'Let me tell you something: I don't want special help. I want to go home.

'OK, I know I'm not the only one with problems. I know now that Auntie Nadia needs help too. And Peter (though I wouldn't want to be the one to tell him). But if (this is what the clown thinks—not me!) your plan is for me to help Auntie Nadia and Peter by staying here, then I'm sorry to say, God, you've added up two and two and made five.

'All I have done since coming here is make matters worse. I have deceived Auntie Nadia and not brought Peter to the Rescue Circus. When Auntie Nadia finds out (as she is likely to do inside the next ten minutes) she will realise that her niece is just one more person who can't be trusted. Probably the same awful mysterious thing will happen to me as happened to Uncle Joe. I'm not saying I won't deserve it. I know now that I was wrong to lend Peter money. I never even asked him what he wanted it for. Now I think it was to run away (it's six o'clock, God, and he still hasn't come home). You might say he won't get very far on five pounds, especially with his appetite, but I've worked out that he's probably got fifteen. I mean, does it seem likely to you that Auntie Nadia would lose her milk money?

'I suppose way deep down I feel ashamed of myself. I hate to think what Auntie Nadia is going to say when she realises that Peter has gone. You wouldn't think it, but underneath, she cares for him. She does—she really does. . . .

'I can hear her now in the kitchen. It sounds like she's scraping something into the pedal-bin. Our tea probably.

'Oh God, I won't mind if you forget everything else I've said in this letter. Just please, please, please make Peter come home!'

CHAPTER SIX

What was that buzz in the distance? Tracy dug her nails into her palms, listening intently. Hope surged within her as the buzz became an unmistakable roar. Brian the Brave's motorbike. But was Peter on the back? She pressed her nose against the window. Oh joy! Five hundred yards down the road she saw a sight more welcome than a row of red stars for spellings: her cousin's spindly, dismounting figure, topped by a huge crash helmet.

'Thanks a million, God!' she scrawled at the bottom of her letter.

Casually, thirty seconds later, she strolled into the kitchen to hold Auntie Nadia's attention until he was safely inside.

'Peter's back,' she announced. 'Helping the clown must've taken longer than he expected. Is the tea all right?'

Auntie Nadia shrugged. 'I threw the spaghetti out. Still, we can have the sauce with French bread, I suppose.'

'Mmmm,' Tracy nodded encouragingly. 'Lovely.'

A smile, like a wary butterfly, flickered at the corners of her aunt's lips. 'And if you look in the fridge you'll find a little ... er ... treat.' She stumbled over the word.

Wide-eyed, Tracy went to the fridge. Opening the door, she found a spotless interior as beautifully ordered as everything else in the house. Dairy products in tupperware boxes lined the top shelf. More plastic boxes filled with lettuce and tomatoes sat neatly underneath. They hadn't been there yesterday as far as Tracy could remember. She felt a twinge of disappointment. If this was Auntie Nadia's idea of spoiling herself, no wonder she had about as many curves as a knitting needle. Tracy was just about to reach for the salad container and try to sound pleased, when she spotted the brown and gold tub beside the low-fat milk in the bottom compartment. Ah! With a gasp of genuine delight, she wrapped her hands round it—cold, curved and mouth-watering.

'Chocolate chip ice-cream! My favourite! Oh, Auntie Nadia, how did you guess?'

The smile flickered again. 'I didn't. Well, I mean ... your mother used to like the stuff. A friend from the church rang up and invited me in for afternoon tea. I don't go out as a rule, but today I did and on the way home I thought I would ... well, you know....'

'Buy ice-cream to celebrate,' finished Tracy. Ooops. She flushed. She hadn't meant to say that.

'Celebrate?' Her aunt peered. 'Celebrate what?'

'Your outing,' Tracy squeaked.

To her great relief, Auntie Nadia didn't seem to find this answer too ridiculous. 'I suppose so,' she sighed gently, running her forefinger along the glistening surface of the tub. 'Do you know, I actually enjoyed myself?'

Tracy nodded. 'I enjoyed myself too.'

The front door slammed.

'We're in the kitchen, Peter,' Tracy called.

Auntie Nadia started ladelling bolognese sauce onto plates. 'About time! Still, it's nice to think of him being helpful for a change. Maybe this Circus of yours isn't such a bad....'

Her voice trailed into silence. She dropped the ladel and stood staring at the doorway with horrified eyes.

Who? Where? What? For a split second Tracy thought that some wild, luminous creature from outer space had barged into Auntie Nadia's kitchen. Then she recognised her cousin. But what had he done to his hair? Four hours ago it had been short, straight and mousey. Now it was an incredible red, brown and gold exclamation mark. Dye—that was it. It was dyed even brighter than Brian the Brave's and Martin the Mighty's.

'You see before you a Hero girded for the final battle,' he roared in his most blood-curdling Cuchulainn voice, flailing a stick around for extra effect. 'The blood of the fallen, the strength of the soil, and the glory of the nations is on my head.' With a whoop he charged in, cracking his birch whip on the table. 'But what I need now is food ... food ... food.' He sat down, pulled the bread towards him and tore off a hunk. Then his eyes alighted on the gold and brown container glistening on the work-top, where Auntie Nadia had left it.

'Nectar fit for the gods!' he whooped. 'Balm to the tongue and stomach after the heat and toil of the day ... ummm.' He looked up at his mother hopefully. 'Any chance of a jug of chocolate sauce to go with it?'

Auntie Nadia did not reply. Deliberately she picked up the tub and removed the lid. Still without speaking she set it in the sink and turned on the hot tap.

'Oh!' Tracy's breath came out in a cross between a sigh and a sob, as the jet of water cut into the marbled brown and cream mould. With a stinging ache at the back of her throat she watched the chocolate chip treat bubble up over the rim of the tub and disappear down the plug-hole.

But it was the look on Auntie Nadia's face that hurt her most. The hard, pale, deathly look as if Peter had walked in and stabbed her.

It was that look which now silenced the Warrior Hero and kept him glued to his chair while the balm to his tongue and stomach washed away.

'It wasn't my fault. I tried to get him to come to the Rescue Circus with me, but he wouldn't. I didn't know he was going to do this, Auntie Nadia. I didn't. Honest,' Tracy cried.

Her aunt seemed neither to see nor hear her. She walked over to the table to stand directly opposite Peter and stare fixedly into his reddening face.

'You are your father's son,' she said quietly and cuttingly, after a prolonged silence. 'You lie to me and deceive me. You steal from me. And now you make a laughing-stock of me in front of the whole city.'

At the mention of his father, Peter's expression changed. All the bravado disappeared from his voice.

'Don't say that. D-dad didn't do anything wrong. He was a hero.'

'Your father—a hero!' Auntie Nadia laughed bitterly. 'He was the worst kind of criminal: the kind who ruins other people's lives for money.'

Peter stuck his fingers in his ears. 'No. No. No,' he moaned. 'You never gave him a chance to explain. You wouldn't even go and visit him. You just believed everything the pigs told you.'

'I believed the evidence,' said Auntie Nadia. 'I understood it as clearly as I now understand the meaning of that ridiculous display on top of your head. You deceived me, didn't you?'

No answer.

'You stole from me. And now you expect me to live in the same house as a boy who looks like a delinquent scarecrow?'

Before she could stop herself, Tracy giggled. It wasn't that she found the conversation funny. She was just so tense that the giggle slipped out in a wobbly gulp. Auntie Nadia cast her a scathing look and continued, her sharp clipped sentences falling like a series of hammer blows.

'You needn't think you're going to use me the way your father did. Once is enough. I had hoped to avoid this, but now I see I have no alternative: I shall sell this house and send you to boarding school.'

Peter looked stunned. He swallowed. 'No one will buy it. I won't let them,' he gulped.

'I'm sure that in the light of the development plans for the area I shall get a very good price.'

'Development plans?' Boom. Another body blow. Tracy saw it was just as Jimbo suspected. Her cousin hadn't a clue about the leisure park.

Coldly and clearly Auntie Nadia explained. By the time she had finished, the very colour of Peter's hair seemed to have faded.

'But ... but ... it's Red Branch land,' he cried weakly. 'The Knights....'

'The Knights, as you call them, will abandon their childish nonsense the minute you're safely out of the way,' interjected Auntie Nadia. 'Now go to your room.'

He went.

Tracy couldn't help feeling sorry for him. Of course he deserved punishment. But to lose his home and his friends (even if they were awful), and to learn his father was a criminal all in five minutes seemed pretty stiff. If she had dyed her hair, her mum would have made her wash it about twenty times, and stopped her pocket money. Of course Auntie Nadia was different: fiercer ... steelier ... less predictable ... shyly confiding one minute and like a tiger stripping flesh from a carcass the next.

And suddenly Tracy stopped feeling sorry for her cousin and felt worried for herself. Auntie Nadia wouldn't just blame Peter for what had happened.

She edged her way to the door, hoping to make her escape while her aunt continued to stare, tight-lipped and unseeing, into space. But no sooner had she started to move than the spell broke. Briefly the hard angry stare became focused.

'You might as well pack your things, Tracy,' she said. 'I shall contact your parents and make arrangements for you to stay in Glasgow until their return.'

Without another glance in her niece's direction she stalked through the door and Tracy was left alone in the kitchen to fish a sodden chocolate chip ice-cream tub out of the gleaming sink.

It's what I wanted. I'm leaving. I'm really going home.

Half an hour later she walked along the road, telling herself how pleased she ought to be. But other accusing voices pricked like needles in her head. Her mum's voice, and the clown's. 'Promise to do what your aunt tells you, darling,' her mum had said at the station. 'Talk to Peter. Tell him what happens at the Rescue Circus,' the clown had advised. Well, both would be disappointed in her. She hadn't obeyed Auntie Nadia and she certainly couldn't go anywhere near Peter. There wasn't any point in talking to him about the Rescue Circus now anyway—not when he was confined to the house.

I don't care, she told herself firmly. I'm going home. Nothing else matters.

Round a bend in the road the self-service filling station came into view. A row of flags flapped cheerily along its low, flat roof. Underneath were the usual advertisements for petrol, Coca Cola and groceries. For ice-cream too, Tracy noted with a sigh. She was hungry. She had tried to eat some bolognese sauce after Auntie Nadia left the kitchen, but the colour had reminded her of Peter's hair. She had ended up scraping it into the pedal-bin on top of a gluey ball of spaghetti, feeling that if she didn't get some fresh air quickly she would be sick. Peter had been playing loud marching music on his ghetto blaster at the time, which had made it easy for her to slip out of the house undetected.

For a moment, standing at the gate, she had looked towards the Hump—deserted now, with a pale apricot sun glowing to one side—and its familiar rounded shape had beckoned her. 'Come over and talk to the clown. Tell him what happened,' it seemed to call. But she had turned her back and headed in the direction of the filling station shop. She was tired, and trying to explain to the clown seemed like too much of an effort. As if being caught between a mad cousin and a moping aunt wasn't bad enough, now she had a problem uncle as well. At least when she believed Uncle Joe had died mysteriously, she could feel sorry for him and blame Auntie Nadia. But she didn't know who to blame now. Auntie Nadia had called her uncle a criminal. Peter said he was a hero. Jimbo, she suspected, knew the truth, but wasn't telling. And the clown would probably only complicate things further by talking about God. She was quite sure he wouldn't be pleased to hear she was leaving. In fact he might even want her to beg Auntie Nadia to change her mind. That was the last thing Tracy intended to do. No, she told herself firmly as she entered the shadowy shelter of the flag-lined roof, the only person I'm going to worry about from now on is myself. I don't care who I've let down, and I won't go back to the clown.

She strolled between the pumps, deliberately wiping the Rescue Circus from her mind. Did many people fill up their tanks and zoom off without paying? she wondered idly, savouring the faint smell of fumes as she pushed open the door of the shop. That was why it had a glass front, she supposed: so the owner could spot escaping cars and zoom after them—or at least take down their registration numbers.

Despite the possibility that he could be robbed at any moment, the bald-headed man behind the counter seemed perfectly relaxed and cheerful.

'And what can I get you, young lady?' he enquired with a nod and a smile.

Tracy dug down deep into the corner of her pocket to finger the hard knob of a pound coin wrapped in a paper tissue. It was the last of her holiday savings, but that didn't matter now. She studied the rows of chocolate bars. What she really wanted was something to chew on; something hot, thick and juicy to fill the guilty hungry hole in her middle. Under the circumstances, though, a munch and a crunch would have to do.

'A packet of peanuts and an apple, please,' she smiled.

The shopkeeper's reply was blotted out in an

almighty roar of engines. With a frown of irritation he glanced towards the door. Tracy's smile faded. Her mouth went dry. She grabbed her purchases and shook the coin out of the tissue so that it rolled across the counter with a clunk. 'Umm, give the change to Doctor Barnardo's.' She dashed towards the back of the shop. There was just enough time to position herself behind a rack of books before the door flung open and Brian the Brave and Martin the Mighty strode in.

Trapped, trembling, eyes huge with fear, Tracy studied the Red Branch leaders through her camouflage of mysteries and romances.

'Ten Silk Cut and a packet of Wrigley's,' Brian drawled, while Martin sauntered over to the car accessories to return with a large can.

'How much?' He slammed it on the counter, managing somehow to turn the question into a threat.

They were like identical twins, Tracy decided. Not the cute sort grandmothers cooed over in the street, but the loud overbearing sort who, because there were two of them, always got their own way. They spoke in the same drawl, dressed in the same leathers, walked with the same swagger, smelled of the same stale cigarette smoke and sported the same tomato-sauce-and-mustard coloured rainbows on their heads. The main difference between them, as far as she could see, was their skin. Like the two (much cleaner) youths in the Clearasil advert, Brian had spots and Martin hadn't.

Somewhere behind the counter a telephone rang.

The shopkeeper turned to answer it and Tracy went hot and cold as these twin terrors clumped towards the magazine shelf. Help! They came to a stand-still so close to her hiding-place, she could have reached out and pulled the drooping tail of Martin's tee-shirt.

She watched him lift a couple of racing magazines. 'Cover for me. I want to nick 'em,' he hissed. Brian leaned against the shelf in front of him and he stuffed the magazines down the front of his jacket.

Then, side by side against the ice-cream cabinet, they split the packet of cigarettes between them. Martin struck a match on the heel of his boot and they lit up. The smoke stung Tracy's eyes. She blinked. Her nose itched. Such was the emergency that she forgot she wasn't on speaking terms with God. Please, oh please, she prayed, don't let me sneeze.

'Everything set up for Tweeter's little op?' Martin inhaled deeply.

'His final battle with the Enemy, you mean?' Brian sniggered. 'Sure. Piece of cake. Wonder how Mammy liked his hair!'

Martin's answering smirk revealed two jagged front teeth which made his smooth brown face fractionally more rat-like than Brian's pink spotty one.

'Tweeter's coming on. One of these days he'll do something useful.'

'Yeh. Tomorrow's op will give him a chance to get his baby hands dirty.'

'And it'll give us something to remind him of if he ever steps out of line.'

'Tweeter step out of line! Not likely. Feed him the right story and he'd blow up Buckingham Palace.' Brian lifted the can at his feet and patted it fondly, while Martin funnelled a stream of smoke through the gap in his teeth.

The shopkeeper hung up. He strolled out from behind the counter into the main body of the shop, apparently to straighten the magazines but really, Tracy knew, to show Martin and Brian he had his eye on them. They took the hint and swaggered towards the door.

A wave of relief washed over her. But just as she felt the glorious freedom to reach for her tissue and blow her nose, the kindly shopkeeper landed her right back into the middle of the nightmare.

'Aren't those books a bit old for you, love?' he remarked in his loud, cheerful voice. 'There's comics down the other end.'

Immediately Brian and Martin turned round.

Tracy froze. Please don't let them recognise me. Please don't let them. . . .

But they had. Martin was nudging Brian, pointing and murmuring something in his ear-ringed ear. Brian's eyes narrowed and he nodded. Then, side by side, they left the shop.

CHAPTER SEVEN

Brian the Beast and Martin the Mean: those were the nicknames Tracy would have chosen for the Red Branch leaders. Brave and mighty, my foot, she thought as their motorbikes roared away from the garage in a cloud of exhaust fumes. What mean beastly thing were they planning for tomorrow night? What mean beastly thing might they do to her now that they knew she knew about their plans?

Licking lips that had become dryer than ever, she came out of her hiding-place.

'Anything the matter, love?' The shopkeeper read her anxious face.

Silly old bat. If it hadn't been for him and his big mouth nothing *would* have been the matter—or at least nothing more than before. 'It's just that I don't read comics,' she muttered crossly, pushing her way through the door.

Outside, the stillness took her by surprise. No sound of motorbikes. No passing cars. Even the flags had stopped flapping. She looked down the road as far as the bend, and saw nothing but a gentle array of patchwork hills studded with golden bursts of gorse. No beasts. No meanies. She drank it in, washed over once again by a sense of relief. Nothing bad is going to happen till tomorrow, she found herself thinking. And by that time—joyfully she bit into her apple—I'll be on my way to Scotland.

Deep in thought she munched her way towards the bend. She would tell Auntie Nadia what she'd heard as soon as she got home, she decided. That way she could make doubly sure that Peter (or Tweeter, as his leaders jeeringly called him behind his back) would be kept in his room the following day, while his cousin hopped onto the bus for the ferry. And Brian the Beast and Martin the Mean could plot and swagger and swear till their leathers wore out. They wouldn't be able to catch her.

She flung her apple core defiantly over the hedge, bolder and happier than she had been for weeks. Then, just as quickly, her new-found courage shrivelled to the size of a pip. Oh yes, the scene on the other side of the bend was as peaceful as ever. There was no noise apart from a drowsy chirping of birds. But now she saw the motorbikes, abandoned— two huge black sinister gashes in the hedge.

For a long moment she stared at them, knowing, yet not knowing, what they meant. Brian and Martin. But where?

She started to run.

Immediately, a few hundred metres ahead of her, the two burly figures stepped out of a gateway, blocking her path. She darted across the road. They followed, still heading her off, forcing her to turn down a lane to the right. She ran as hard as her legs would carry her, faster than she had ever run before in her life. And still they came: two relentless pairs of lungs and boots calling and thundering behind her, while her own lungs ached and pounded halfway up her throat, so she couldn't even scream.

She knew even before they grabbed her that she had no chance of escape. Still she kicked, yelled, squirmed and wriggled as they hauled her over the quarry gate.

At the height of the struggle her teeth encountered Brian's thumb.

'Yoww!' he shrieked, letting go for a moment to stick it under his arm-pit and hop round on one leg. 'Stinking little vampire.'

Her satisfaction was short-lived. Martin seized her hands and tied them behind her back. Next her mouth was bound with a dirty rag. Eugh! It smelled like something out of a dustbin. She kicked as strongly as she could until her feet were tied. Then propped against the outside wall of a tumble-down shed, she eyed her captors across her gag, bruised, exhausted and very very scared.

'Don't like spies, do we Bri'?' Martin smiled rattishly at Brian who was still nursing his thumb.

'Not half. Especially that one,' his spotty companion hissed between grimaces.

'Trouble with spies is they can louse things up. And we don't want any tell-tales interfering with tomorrow's op, do we Bri'?'

Again Brian shook his head and glared.

'So we're going to open up this nice damp shed for you and lock you inside. Then tomorrow, if everything goes smoothly, we'll come and let you out again.'

'We will?' Brian clearly didn't think much of that idea.

'Of course, we'll have to make sure you don't tell any tales,' Martin continued in the same light, mocking tone. 'That's why we're taking your watch and sweat-shirt.' His voice hardened. 'Then if you breathe a word to anyone, those are the clues the police will find at the scene of the op. And guess who'll end up before the magistrate? Now what do you say to that, eh?'

All she could manage was a few hoarse croaking noises in the back of her throat.

'Sounds like a sick parrot, don't she?' Martin sniggered as he unstrapped her watch.

Brian continued to glower. With a shudder of fear, Tracy realised that he was searching for a way to get back at her. As if being chased, tied up and threatened with a night in a cold damp shed wasn't bad enough.

Suddenly his scowl lifted. A gleam appeared in his pink-rimmed eyes.

'Chop off her hair,' he said eagerly.

Tracy croaked, gasped and almost choked on the rag. No, no, not my hair, she screamed inwardly. Her hair was special. Everyone said so. It was long and thick and the colour of Highland toffee, streaked with cream by the sun. Today, like most other days, she had swept it up in a high pony-tail. It had tumbled down in the struggle and now hung loosely across her shoulder in a tangled bunch.

'What use would that be?' Martin enquired, catching the bunch between nicotine-stained fingers and tugging.

'Don't like it. Don't like *her*,' Brian growled.

'So you want to play barber?' A teasing note crept into Martin's voice. 'Do you think you'll like her more without it?'

Brian couldn't take teasing any better than he could take a pain in his thumb. He swore furiously and threw a punch at Martin's chest. Martin let go of Tracy's hair and for a second she thought there would be a fight.

But next moment he was slapping his partner on the back. 'See this fella? He's a pure genius.'

Brian stopped swearing and brightened.

'He's right. Dead right. Of course we've gotta chop it off. Gotta give you a reason for being out all night. Tweeter's ma might start asking awkward questions, mightn't she? You know what will happen if you breathe one word about us. So we do you a favour. We give you an excuse. This way you can say you was scared to come home in case people didn't fancy your new hair-do.'

Brian leered. He fished a large metallic pen-knife out of his jacket pocket with one hand, and grabbed Tracy's pony-tail in the other. 'Nice one, Marty. I'll chop. You keep her still.'

Screams of desperation filled the girl's head. Help me, oh help me, help me. Martin was holding her. He was tightening the gag. She couldn't move. Or breathe. Heart pounding, she watched Brian unsheath the rusty blade. Any minute now he would start sawing through the wreckage of her pony-tail. She shut her eyes. She couldn't bear it. Was this how people felt long ago when they had legs and arms cut off without anaesthetic? It was cruel ... so cruel. And no one would understand. They'd think she'd done it on purpose. Oh help me, help me!

She could never quite recall what happened next. Perhaps the rescue came about so fast that her brain couldn't keep up. All she knew was that one minute the screams were inside her head and the next they were all around her. Screams, yells, shouts, curses, together with a ferocious barking and snarling. Only this time the Beast and the Meanie were the ones shrieking for help. Her panic was theirs. Hounded by a howling fury of teeth and tails, they were running, stumbling, throwing themselves across the rough stoney quarry surface towards the quarry gate.

And the clown was there. He had come racing towards her through the hedge, accompanied by a Jimbo so beside himself with rage, the stubble had turned to bristle on his head.

'If I could get my hands on those ... those ... those....' He sounded as if he was about to explode.

'Here. Help me untie her,' Carlo did not even glance at her fleeing tormentors. He was kneeling beside her, removing the filthy gag.

'Tracy,' he said softly. 'Are you all right?'

'Hello,' she croaked.

'Hello yourself.'

She saw the concern in his sea-blue eyes. She tried to stand, but her legs were like jelly.

'Hold tight.' He picked her up as easily as if she had been a very small child. Then he carried her all the way from the quarry in his arms.

If you had to have a fright, the nicest place in the whole world to recover, Tracy discovered, was in the clown's caravan. 'Not a word,' he had warned Jimbo. 'Not a single question, until she's warmed up and you've cooled down and I've made hot chocolate.'

He had set her down on the divan seat under the window with three pillows for her back, a light, fluffy rug for her feet and a steaming bowl of water for her face and hands. Jimbo was given the job of feeding the dogs outside. Through the open window she could hear his louder-than-necessary comments as he patted their heaving flanks.

'Well done, fellas. You sorted that lot out. Got a mouthful of Martin's Wranglers, did you, Goliath? Good on yer. Have a sausage.'

She couldn't help smiling. Still, she was glad Carlo didn't expect her to talk. He had busied himself at the stove, pouring milk into a sturdy saucepan, adjusting the blue gas flame. He seemed preoccupied—as if his eyes were focused on something beyond the immediate task. Yet he did not seem to be thinking about the drama of the past half an hour. His face looked far too peaceful for that. In fact the whole caravan was peaceful. Tracy lay back on her pillows remembering how she had felt when she first came into the Rescue Circus tent. She felt the same now. As if she had entered another world; a world where beasts, meanies, mad cousins, unpredictable aunts and problem uncles ceased to exist, where nothing horrible could ever happen again.

She was tempted to close her eyes and let her

81

mind drift, but that would have meant losing out on an ideal opportunity to inspect the clown's caravan in detail. It wasn't just that she wanted to be able to describe it to her friends when she got home, she wanted to see what it would tell her about the clown. The places people lived in always said something about their owners. 'You know a lazy lion by its den,' was the way her mum put it, meaning usually that Tracy's bedroom had turned into a jungle of toys and clothes.

There was nothing junglish about Carlo's den. Every bit of available space had been put to good use. He's well-organised, Tracy deduced, peering round the shelves, Auntie Nadia-style, to see what else she could learn. The most obvious message came from the books. There were rows of them—paperbacks, hardbacks, no-backs, ranging over every topic under the sun, from *The House At Pooh Corner* to *Sheep-farming in Southern Australia*. Deduction two: the clown likes reading and he picks up books in second-hand bookshops. Other deductions followed: there was the long thin compartment between cupboards which held three rackets and told her the clown played squash; the row of colourful herbs and spices above the cooker which suggested that his cooking skills were not limited to bacon butties; and finally the tool-box, stowed away under the table on top of a stack of wooden planks, announcing loud and clear why everything slotted so compactly into place. The clown was a handyman. He must have designed and built most of those shelves, cupboards and compartments himself.

Lucky, lucky Carlo, Tracy thought. Imagine being able to stay somewhere as nice as this all the year round. If he had been in a talking mood she would have asked him to tell her how long he'd been on the road, and whether he thought there was any chance of her living in a caravan one day herself. But though the milk was in the saucepan and he was now measuring heaped spoonfuls of chocolate powder into mugs, his eyes still requested silence.

There was one more thing she could tell without asking. This two-wheeled home was far from new. Caravans these days were made of light materials for easy towing. You wouldn't tow this van anywhere in a hurry. Its doors were thick. Its seats and tables had clearly been made to last. There were heavy brass handles on the drawers and a gleaming copper canopy above the stove. Everything, in fact, seemed chunky, strong and well-worn—like the clown himself.

Congratulating herself on her detective work (perhaps she would write about it for her Brownie Wide Awake Challenge), Tracy sank deeper into her pillows. But next minute she was bolt upright, shattering the silence with a squeal: 'Carlo, your bowler hat! It *moved*!'

Instantly the clown was at her side, unshockable as ever.

'I daresay,' he replied, a slow grin spreading from ear to ear.

It seemed to Tracy that he couldn't have heard correctly. 'I'm talking about your hat. The one you wore on Sunday. I saw it walk across the seat.'

'You can't go believing everything you see!'

She opened her mouth, but he stemmed the tide of protest, lifting the bowler with a flourish.

'The hat didn't walk—just the body underneath.'

She found herself staring at a melon-sized mound of black and tan fluff.

'Scruffy, Scruffy, here boy!' she laughed. But to her disappointment the little dog didn't spring to life with his usual mischievous prance. He looked up just long enough to lick the clown's hand with a small pink tongue, then buried his head back under his tail.

'He's tired, I suppose,' Tracy sighed.

'Hmmm.' The clown seemed puzzled. 'Never seen him like that before. He's off his food too.'

'Maybe you should take him to the vet.'

'That's an idea. If he doesn't pick up by tomorrow.' Affectionately the clown fondled the shaggy head under his hand. Again, the only response came from the small pink tongue.

'Oh dear,' Tracy frowned. 'He *doesn't* look well.'

They were still considering Scruffy's health when the caravan door burst open.

'Hey, mind yer cow-juice!' Jimbo yelled.

He dived for the stove and grabbed the saucepan— just in time to save its frothy contents from the flames.

At last the hot chocolate was ready. They sat round the table sipping the dark sweet brew. Such was the soothing effect of this two-wheeled world that Tracy had almost forgotten about her fright. And when

Jimbo eventually reminded her of it, frowning into his mug and vowing to 'sort them Red Branch swine out good and proper', she heard herself say something unexpected.

'I suppose it was partly my own fault.'

'Eh? Whatcher mean?' Jimbo wiped his mouth with the back of his hand.

'Well,' she continued carefully. 'If I'd come here first to talk to Carlo, I wouldn't have been in the shop, so I wouldn't have overheard Brian and Martin's plans, so they wouldn't have thought I was a spy, so they wouldn't have attacked me. I'd have been all right then, wouldn't I?'

Jimbo looked at her in amazement.

'So? If me parents had gone with me granny to America, me dad wouldn't be on the dole, so he could afford to buy me a racer. I'd be all right then too.'

He didn't understand, but Carlo did. She could tell from the way he leaned back in his seat, nodding soberly.

'What was it you wanted to tell me?'

'It was about Peter.' She took a deep breath, then launched into her story, her voice growing higher and faster with every phrase. 'I would have told him about the leisure centre, but I didn't get a chance. Auntie Nadia beat me to it. It was awful. I've never seen her so angry. He'd dyed his hair, you see. And now he's being sent to boarding school. And Auntie Nadia's selling the house. And I'm going home. And....'

'Steady on there. Steady on.' Calmly the clown

reached for the saucepan and refilled her mug. 'Let's take this again from the beginning. What exactly happened when you went back to the house?'

More slowly this time Tracy told her tale. It was hard, very hard. She felt uncomfortable about her own part in the deception, and she didn't enjoy remembering the look on Auntie Nadia's face. Or Peter's face, for that matter—especially when he heard his father described as a criminal.

'If only I even knew what Auntie Nadia meant.' She looked up at the clown, her eyes clouded over with the mystery and confusion of it all. 'I mean up till today I thought Uncle Joe was dead. Now I don't know what to believe. I just wish *someone* would tell me the truth.'

The someone she had in mind was Jimbo. He was trying to look as if he hadn't heard, absently pulling at one ear-lobe.

'Do you know anything about Tracy's uncle?' the clown prompted.

The ear-lobe became very red.

'Well?'

'Everyone knows,' the lad exploded. 'Sure, wasn't it splashed all over the papers when it happened? Why should I be the one to tell her?'

'Because you are here and everyone else isn't—thankfully!' smiled the clown.

And so, at long last, and not without a good deal of prodding and prompting from the clown, Tracy learned the truth. It was even worse than she had suspected: Uncle Joe *was* a criminal. But until the dreadful day three years ago, when the police

86

had come to the house and charged him, no one had known anything of his drug-dealing past. He had been tried and imprisoned. As if this wasn't bad enough, Auntie Nadia had learned at the trial that she wasn't, as she had always believed, his first wife. He had been married before, under a different name.

'What!' Tracy's mind reeled with shock. 'You mean my uncle was married to two women at the same time?'

'Course not.' Jimbo shook his head energetically, as if relieved to be able to say something in the criminal's favour. 'He divorced the first one, didn't he? Gave her up with the pushing, see.'

Tracy saw. She saw why her aunt didn't go out, why she had torn up her wedding pictures and refused to visit Uncle Joe in prison, why—most importantly—she wanted someone to keep an eye on her son.

'Poor, poor Auntie Nadia! No wonder she doesn't trust people. She must spend her time worrying in case Peter gets into trouble too,' was what she said. 'Which is just what he's about to do,' she added, suddenly remembering the conversation she had overheard in the shop.

Jimbo made her go over the details again. 'Brian and Martin! What did I tell you? Up to all the slimy rotten tricks of the day.' His eyes sparkled when he grasped the full picture. 'But we'll put a stop to their scheming. Oh yes, we'll show those Red Branch roosters a thing or two.'

'I can't think how.' Tracy's heart began beating

wildly. 'I mean we can't go to the police. We don't even know what they've planned.'

'Who needs police?' Jimbo puffed out his chest. 'I've got mates, haven't I? My lot'll be onto those Red Branch creeps first thing tomorrow morning. We won't let them out of our sight.'

'But what if they attack you?'

'We'll kill 'em,' crowed Jimbo gleefully. 'Not your cousin, of course. You gotta make sure he's out of the way.'

Tracy nodded. 'As long as Auntie Nadia makes him stay in the house until he goes to boarding school, everything will be all right.'

'Will it?' said the clown.

She knew by the set of his lips that he didn't agree.

But why did he have to be disapproving? Couldn't he see that this was the best they could do?

'Sending Peter to boarding school isn't going to change things,' he continued in the same quiet serious tone. 'Not the important things, anyway. He's as likely to get into trouble there as he is here. More so, in fact.'

'If he does, it won't be my fault!' Tracy flashed.

'Won't it?' said the clown.

He had put his finger gently yet unerringly on her guilty spot. The hateful possibility she had so firmly put out of her mind. What if God wanted her to act? Would she be willing, if that was the only way?

'But what can *I* do?' she almost wailed.

'You can bring Peter to see me first thing tomorrow morning.'

'No I can't. Auntie Nadia won't let either of us out of the house.'

'Talk to her. Tell her you're sorry. Say how important it is.'

'But even if she agrees, Peter won't. He hates you. He'll just scive off with Martin and Brian.'

'Say that I've something important to tell him— something he'll really want to hear.'

She looked at him pityingly and shook her head. How little he understood her cousin. 'He won't want to hear about God, Carlo. All he cares about is humps and battles and food.'

'He cares about his father.'

She remembered the look on Peter's face, the note of longing in his voice, as he protested that her uncle was a hero. Yes, in spite of everything, he *did* care about his dad.

'So what's that got to do with it?' she muttered.

'Everything.' The clown grasped her shoulders and stared into her face, as if what he was trying to convey went deeper than words. 'You see there's been a most amazing coincidence.'

Here we go. She looked back at him with eyes that asked the obvious question, but did not plan to be impressed. 'Well?'

'Part of my work is visiting prisons. Holding meetings. Talking to prisoners. Three months ago a man came to me after a meeting and we had a long conversation.'

89

'So?'

'The name just came back to me there as Jimbo was talking. Joseph Richards, father of Peter Richards, or as you call him,' his voice rang out gladly, 'Uncle Joe.'

CHAPTER EIGHT

Tracy burst into her bedroom and flopped down at her desk, her face flushed with success. Her mind was buzzing. Thoughts and questions jumped about like grasshoppers. With a wriggle of excitement, she reached for the airmail pad.

'Dear God,' she scribbled eagerly. 'You probably know all about this already, but I am telling you because I need to tell someone and the only other person who understands is the clown—and he's not here (lucky him!).

'I have just done something very brave.

'I shall begin from the time I was trying to make up my mind about doing it; when Carlo waved me off from the doorstep of his peaceful caravan before going back inside to do whatever he does at nine o'clock at night—put up a couple of shelves maybe, or read about sheep-farmers in Australia. He had wanted to walk back to Auntie Nadia's with me, but I said he mustn't leave Scruffy (who's sick) and anyway I had Jimbo. Of course I couldn't let Jimbo come too close to the house in case Auntie Nadia noticed and got the wrong idea. So we said goodbye at the bottom of the lane. I was already thinking so hard about my decision, I ran the rest of the way on my own, no bother. At home, my mum has a poster in the kitchen which says: "How to get rid of little problems. Have big problems." And it's true.

'The first thing I heard when I opened the front door was the sound of the vacuum cleaner in the living-room. I knew it couldn't be Peter vacuuming, God, because he thinks housework means the house clearing itself up behind him. (He wouldn't last five minutes in Brownies!) So that told me I didn't need to worry about Auntie Nadia. Would you believe, though, I almost wished she had been standing there in the hallway with a face like an iceberg, not giving me a chance to open my mouth before ordering me to my room. At least then I would have had an A1 excuse for chickening out.

'As it was, there was nothing to stop me except the screwed-up, thumping feeling in my tummy. I sent up an emergency prayer then—remember? I asked you to help me know what to say to Peter and not to let him kick me.

'When I think back over what happened I am amazed. (You did help, didn't you?) I went up those stairs, and instead of turning right into my bedroom, I turned left into his. I didn't knock or anything. I just opened the door and went in.

'Gosh! What a mess! The room was covered in heaps: chest-drawers, jeans, bedclothes, tapes, posters, and there, in the middle, my cousin—the biggest heap of all—wrapped round his Cuchulainn book.

'When he looked up, I almost ran away. His face was all fierce and swollen and blotchy, like the scarey masks you see in the shops at Hallowe'en, topped by a horrible blotchy mass of hair. But he didn't get up and kick me. So I stayed.

'I asked him what part he was reading (it was the only thing I could think of to say).

'"Cuchulainn's fight to the death," he growled.

'"Oh." I put my head on one side, trying to look as if I wanted to hear more.

'"Go on, barbarian. Admit it," he sneered. "You haven't a clue how he died."

'"Ummm ... heroically?" I thought that was a pretty safe bet.

'I was right. The idea seemed to send him into a sort of trance. He stopped sneering and started rocking backwards and forwards with his knees pulled up so the book was pressed against his chest, chanting a description. I can't remember the exact words now, but they were something about how Cuchulainn died in battle, defending his honour and the honour of Ulster and the honour of his race. And how he slaughtered the men of Erin in their thousands, leaving their red bones scattered like banks of buttercups across the plain.

'Buttercups, God! I ask you! But you know, as I watched him hunched up there in the middle of the floor, rocking backwards and forwards like a zombie, for once I didn't think he was talking nonsense. I saw behind the words. The clown had been right. Boarding school wasn't going to be the answer.

Auntie Nadia might succeed in getting Peter there, but he was planning to fight until the very end. And all the time, no matter what terrible things he did or how unhappy he made people, he would think he was a hero.

'I wished then I could get him to stand in front of a mirror and see how small, weird and blotchy he really was. But I didn't think there was much chance of that. So I tried to hit on something—*anything*—that would bring him out of his trance.

'I knew I couldn't barge straight in and say: "Peter, the clown wants to see you about your dad." In fact I didn't know how I was going to bring the subject round. I just opened my mouth and the words came. (Now I'm wondering, God, did you put them there?)

'"Peter," I said. "I'd really like to see what Uncle Joe looks like. Have you got a photo?"

'The effect was like turning on a light. He stopped rocking immediately. His hands fell to his sides and he stared at me as if I'd told him he'd won some fantastic prize in a competition and he could hardly believe his ears.

'"He looks like what he is—a hero," he said.

'"So show me then," I said back, one eye on his face and the other on his feet.

'So he did.

'God, you'll never *guess* where Peter keeps his father's photo.

'Sellotaped onto the back page of his Cuchulainn book!

'Seeing it, I felt more confused than ever. (I also

saw why he got so upset when Auntie Nadia tore the book up and threw it into the pedal-bin on top of the peelings.) Uncle Joe *does* look like a hero. He's tall, with blond hair and smiling eyes and a beard. He reminded me of Good King Wenceslas in my carol book. You could just imagine him all dressed in purple velvet with a crown on his head going out in the snow to feed poor people. He also looked as if he could tell brilliant bedtime stories.

'I didn't say anything and I suppose I didn't need to, because Peter could see I was impressed.

'"So now you know," he growled (but not fiercely) and slapped the book shut.

'"Do you miss him very much?" I said.

'He turned his head away from me then. I think perhaps he was trying not to cry. Anyway, I didn't wait for an answer. I went on. "How would you like it if someone could give him a message from you and maybe even bring one back from him?"

'He still didn't answer. He just opened the book again and stared at the picture. And this time a tear definitely plopped down onto the page.

'"It could be fixed up, you know," I said.

'"HOW?" (I'm putting that in capitals to show he shouted.)

'Of course I didn't shout back. "I'll tell you in a minute," I said quietly. "But first I need to know: would you do anything, anything at all, to get in contact with your dad?"

'He clenched his fists and screwed up his face. "Anything. *Anything*," he said.

'"Well," I said slowly, "I just happen to know

95

someone who goes round visiting prisons. And he just happens to be pretty friendly with your dad. And there's things your dad told him on his last visit that he would like to tell you. So he wants me to bring you to see him."

'Peter looked straight at me then, the same way our neighbours' dog looks when they're about to give him his dinner.

'"Yes," he sort of panted. "Yes. Yes. Who is it?"

'I knew then I'd been clever as well as brave. You must admit, God, no one could have got round to the point more cleverly than I did. "It's the clown," I said. "He asked me to ask you if you would visit his caravan tomorrow morning. Will you come?"

'Of course I was expecting him to say yes. But do you know, after all my cleverness, the eager look just disappeared from his face. The blotches joined up so that it was the colour of a pillar box. "I can't," he squawked like a strangled hen.

'I could have kicked him.

'Then I thought: maybe it's because of Auntie Nadia. Probably he thinks she won't let him out of the house. I saw I was going to have to do something even braver than I'd already done.

'"If you're worried about your mum," I said, "I'll speak to her. I'll tell her we're both really sorry about what happened and that nothing like that will ever happen again. I'll ask her to let you come out of your room and to let me not go home after all. But you've got to promise—hero's honour," I looked at him really meaningfully, "that you won't go off anywhere else without me and that you won't be involved in any ops."

'That startled him. His face went GPO red again, and I could see he was wondering how much I knew.

'"I know more than you think," I said firmly. "You've got a choice, Peter. Between your gang and your father. Which is it going to be?"

'He got up and went to the window then, and stared out at the Hump.

'"That van has no right to be there," he growled, taking deep breaths and clenching and unclenching his fists.

'I could see he was trying to work himself up into one of his stupid battle frenzies. I grabbed the Cuchulainn book, flipped it open at the back page and shoved it under his nose. "That van belongs to a friend of your dad's," I said. "And he wants to see us first thing tomorrow."

'He looked down at the photo, and little by little the madness drained out of him until he was just like a normal boy (apart from his hair). He stared at the picture and suddenly seemed to make up his mind.

'"If we go first thing, we'll be in time," he said in a gruff voice with a wobble at the end. Then he looked at the door and the wobble got worse. "But what about Mum?"

'I wasn't sure what he meant about being in time. (For orange and biscuits, probably, knowing him.) But I did understand about Auntie Nadia.

'"Don't worry. I'll talk her round," I said.

'So now you know, God. That's the story so far. I came straight back into my room, leaving Peter among the heaps. I would like to tell you he had turned over a new leaf and had started putting his jeans and socks and T-shirts back into drawers, but that would be an exaggeration. He did seem to be thinking, though. And he wasn't reading his Cuchulainn book, which must be a good sign.

'Anyway, I suppose I'd better finish this letter and go and speak to Auntie Nadia. The noise of the vacuum cleaner has stopped, but I think she's still in the dining-room. Lying with her eyes closed, probably. Worrying about Peter. Probably her tummy is in knots, just like mine is, only her knots are tighter and seem to be there all the time.

'But that doesn't stop me feeling worried for myself. Like I said before, it's all right for the clown, moving from place to place in his peaceful caravan, getting all the miracles, while I take the risks.

'What's going to happen, I would like to know, if I persuade Auntie Nadia to let me stay and give Peter another chance, and then, tomorrow, after seeing the clown, he just goes and gets involved with the Beast and the Meanie all over again? They have it in for me. Especially Brian. When I think how close his knife got to my pony-tail, I feel sick—and that was *before* I'd loused anything up. If Peter turns round and breaks his promise, I could lose my whole scalp.

'Before I change my mind I will write down three reasons why I am going to go through with this, hair or no hair:

'(1) Because of Carlo. He has a cushy time of it, but there is still something special about him and he makes you real (even without talking). Also he rescued me from Martin and Brian so I owe him one.

'(2) Because of Auntie Nadia. I want to make up for letting her down. (That's just reminded me of something the clown said when I was sitting wondering how any uncle of mine could behave so badly. He said that Uncle Joe really loved Auntie Nadia and had never wanted to hurt her.)

'(3) Because of you. I learned something today. I learned that doing what I want instead of what you want doesn't pay off in the end. Today I thought the safest thing for me to do was to go to the shop and not to the clown's caravan. But I was wrong. Now part of me (the tummy knotted part) thinks that the safest thing would be for me not to go anywhere near Auntie Nadia, but the part that remembers what the clown said thinks differently. So I'm giving you another chance, God. I'm trusting you, like we heard this afternoon, not to let me down. Yours hopefully. Tracy MacA. Amen.

'PS. Sorry for my last letter. I was in a bad mood at the time.'

Auntie Nadia was not stretched out on the settee. Tracy came into the living-room to find her reaching up to the top row of latticed window frames, scrubbing round the edges with a toothbrush. The light of the spot-lamp by which she worked sent her elongated shadow leaping up the right-hand wall of

99

the room—like a lonely runner-bean, the girl thought, with no chance of being picked.

Nervously she cleared her throat. 'Excuse me, Auntie Nadia.'

The beanstalk on the wall jerked violently.

'Oh!' With a gasp, her aunt spun round. 'Tracy! What do you mean creeping up on me like that? Can't you see I'm busy?'

It wasn't a very promising beginning. One major difference between her cousin and her aunt, Tracy now saw, was that Peter pulled things apart when he was upset and didn't mind company, while Auntie Nadia deliberately hid herself away with her brushes, buckets and dusters.

'I just ... er ... wanted to speak to you,' she stammered.

'Well?' The tone indicated that she'd better be quick.

'I just ... um....' Tracy focused on the patch of carpet at her feet where the pile had been freshly vacuumed the wrong way. This conversation was going the wrong way too. 'I just ... um ... wanted to say that I'm sorry. And so's Peter,' she muttered.

Her aunt turned back to work. 'If I've learned one lesson in life it's this,' she said bitterly. 'Being sorry doesn't change things.'

'Oh, but it does if the people who are sorry don't do whatever they are sorry for ever again.' Tracy began to gain confidence. 'And we won't. Honestly. I'll stay with Peter every minute of every day from now till the end of the holidays.'

'That won't be necessary,' came the cold reply.

'Peter will be going to boarding school and I have been in touch with your father's cousin in Glasgow to arrange for your return. You'll be leaving tomorrow.'

If anyone had told Tracy twenty-four hours earlier that she would be upset to hear those words, she wouldn't have believed them. But now they hit her like an icy shower.

'Please, Auntie Nadia,' she begged, her hands pressed together. 'Please give us a second chance.'

'Certainly not.' Her aunt's scrubbing became so violent, Tracy was afraid she would crack the pane. 'I don't give anyone more than one chance to make my life a misery. And in any case, children who deceive and steal as you did must expect to be punished.'

'Oh, I'm not asking you to let us off altogether,' the girl cried. 'I mean Peter will pay you back out of his pocket money and I'll do anything you want. Only please can we go to the Rescue Circus tomorrow morning. It's ever so important. Boarding school isn't the right punishment for him, you see. The clown expects he'll just go from bad to worse.'

The toothbrush fell onto the window-sill with a clatter, making the beanstalk figure on the wall look as if it had shed its only pod.

'How dare he,' was all Auntie Nadia said—all she needed to say in that awful rasping tone.

'I'm s-sorry . . . truly,' Tracy bleated. 'I mean . . . oh dear . . . this has all gone wrong.'

Upstairs once more, she sat at her desk, blinking back tears. The three pages of her last letter to God lay scattered at her elbow.

'It's all gone wrong,' she muttered again. 'Why didn't you help with Auntie Nadia? What's the good of Peter being ready to speak to the clown if she won't let him? What's the good of me taking risks if she just ends up angrier than ever?'

Tracy was too hurt, disappointed and confused to put this down on paper. In any case, writing letters to God was a waste of time, she had decided. He never answered properly. With a flick of her pony-tail, she gathered the flimsy biro-covered sheets and crumpled them into a ball. Then, realising the ball wouldn't fit into her soap-box, she smoothed it flat and folded it into a small square. She took the pink box from her wash-bag, slipped the square inside with the others and sat down again at the window.

It was a windy night. Black clouds rolled across the heavy grey-green back-cloth of the sky, like lumps of unformed clay, blocking the moon. It seemed to Tracy that her hopes for her aunt and cousin had all been blocked out too.

But at ground level, between the Hump and the quarry, a light still burned. Was Carlo making himself another cup of chocolate? she wondered, identifying his van.

Somehow this homely thought was comforting. 'Well,' she imagined herself telling him, 'whatever happens now, it truly isn't my fault. I did my best. I was brave. I was ready to stay if I had to.'

And in her imagination, he nodded his approval, though his eyes remained sad. 'You did your best too,' she added generously. 'I mean, I'm sure you would have helped Peter if he'd come anywhere near you.'

Momentarily the moon peeped out between the shifting lumps of cloud, encouraging her to become more generous still. OK. She wasn't blaming anyone any more—not even God.

Their plan had just gone wrong.

Auntie Nadia had refused to listen. She didn't believe in second chances. And she didn't want help.

With a sigh, Tracy picked up her wash-bag to go to the bathroom and wash before bed. Tomorrow she would catch the ferry. Then Peter would be sent to boarding school (how long before he got himself expelled?) while Auntie Nadia moved from this gloomy, gleaming tissue-box house to somewhere even gloomier, where she could grow angrier, lonelier and thinner than ever.

And there was nothing anyone could do.

CHAPTER NINE

As soon as Tracy came back from the bathroom, she climbed into bed. Within minutes she was soundly asleep. But in her dreams she still sat at the window gazing out at a sky full of clouds. Horrible clouds, they were. The sort she'd seen in Dracula films, thick and sulphurous, writhing like snakes. 'Oh no!' she gasped, as this venomous mass swirled in round the moon. Would they squeeze it out of existence? No. To her relief it simply folded itself into an arrow and shot through their coils. Then, like a bird, it spread its crescent wings and flew to the top of the Hump where it grew full and round as a beachball, before rolling down the hill and across the fields towards the house. Up the lane and round the bend it came, getting nearer and bigger and brighter all the time. Along the road and up the garden path.

'Stop! You're blinding me! Don't come any closer,' she cried, as the glorious silvery moonlight filled her room.

'Don't worry. I won't hurt you,' the moon laughed back.

And peeping through her fingers, she laughed as

well; for, though it had rolled right on in through her window (and who wouldn't feel rather odd with the moon on the end of their bed?) it had found such a funny way to dim its rays.

It had put on a bowler hat.

And then, as suddenly, the laughter and the brightness disappeared. The room went black. Zzzooom. She woke with a jolt, sat up in bed and turned on the bedside lamp. What was that? She listened intently. Only the wind? Or was it the muffled roar of motorbikes in the lane?

A quick glance at the round, normally friendly face of her alarm-clock and she shuddered again. Two o'clock. The 'tomorrow' the Beast and the Meanie had talked about had begun two hours ago. Even though it was still darkest night outside, today was the day of the op.

Ten rapid steps took her from her bedside to the door of Peter's room. She pressed an ear against it, wriggling her toes for warmth as the wind whistled out under the crack at the bottom.

He has a window open, she guessed, with a slight sense of surprise, for usually it was Auntie Nadia who went round opening windows, and Peter who slammed them shut. Perhaps her talk with her cousin earlier that evening had helped him see the merits of fresh air.

'Peter,' she called through the key-hole. 'Peter, can you hear me?'

There was no reply. Either he was sound asleep, or awake but not answering, or else.... The third possibility seemed too horrible to consider, yet too haunting to put out of her mind. Yes, at the risk of sending him into a rage for the rest of her stay, she had to find out.

She opened the door.

A gust of wind hit her, blowing her Snoopy night-shirt close around her knees. 'It's like an igloo in here. You'll catch pneumonia, Peter,' she said bravely and hopefully, and turned on the light.

'Lying lizard!' she muttered bitterly, her worst fears confirmed. The bed was empty. The bedclothes lay in their usual heap, together with a pair of pyjama bottoms, his Cuchulainn book, two empty crisp packets and a half-eaten apple. The packets hadn't blown across the room because the book sat on top of them. And on the bedside table, beneath the open window, she saw another piece of paper, held in place by a stone.

Her first thought was that her cousin had left her a message.

'*Operation Death Hound brung forward 002 hours. Meet bottum lane ten minits,*' she read.

Her heart beat wildly and she felt a flash of anger mixed with amazement. Not only had Peter broken his promise, it seemed he expected her to join him! 'Some hope,' she muttered grimly. And then, study-ing the note more closely she began to wonder. Surely Peter knew how to spell? She grabbed his Cuchulainn book and considered the hand-printed name and address on the front. The lettering was totally different from the note's uneven scrawl. So where had it come from? Of course. The truth hit her with a second windy gust. The Beast and the

Meanie were responsible. They must have thrown it in through the open window wrapped round the stone. (Ah yes! She spotted the elastic band on the floor. Further proof of her theory.) Yes, the message was meant for Peter, not for her—a message from his leaders telling him their operation would take place sooner than planned (probably because they were afraid she would squeak).

And Peter (the skunk!) had slunk out of the house to take part.

She held the piece of paper between both hands and twisted it, wishing it had been her cousin's scrawny neck. So much for his hero's honour! So much for her efforts to keep him out of trouble! So much for the clown's miracle! It just went to show that Auntie Nadia had been right all along. People like Peter didn't deserve second chances.

So what was she meant to do now?

Shoving the piece of paper into the Snoopy's ear pocket of her night-shirt, she crept back into her own room to think.

The most sensible thing, she decided, settling herself cross-legged on top of the bed, was to do nothing. That way she wouldn't run into any more trouble with the Red Branch gang. She would leave the house tomorrow as planned, and the rest would be none of her business. The only block to this course of action was her Brownie duty to stop crime. Of course she didn't know what Operation Death Hound involved. It might be anything—from painting slogans on walls to breaking into the petrol station. But still she knew she ought to let somebody in authority know that something was going on.

One way would be to tell Auntie Nadia. But what if Auntie Nadia got mad with her for not mentioning it sooner? Worse still, what would happen when the Beast and the Meanie found out she'd talked? And find out they would, for Peter would tell them. He was on their side, after all. What if he gave them her home address and they followed her all the way back to Scotland and scalped her!

She sighed. It would be so much easier if she knew exactly what the Knights were planning. Then she could simply slip downstairs to the kitchen and dial 999 on the wall-phone. She wouldn't even have to say who she was. She could be ... what was the name they gave people like her on the news? Yes, that was it ... an anonymous caller. 'Hello. Give me the police, please,' she would say calmly and clearly, the way she'd been taught. 'Hello. Is that the police? Well, this is an anonymous caller just ringing to tell you that ... um....' At this point her imagination ran out. She didn't know what she was ringing to tell the police. That was the whole problem.

With another sigh, she stretched out on the bed and stared at the ceiling. Perhaps thinking back over the Beast and the Meanie's conversation in the shop might give her some clues. Resolutely she ignored the knots in her tummy and forced herself to go over the whole incident in detail: what the Terrible Twins had said to the shopkeeper; what they'd said to each other; the way they'd looked; the things they'd bought....

'Petrol,' she murmured up at the lampshade, remembering the can. So what would they be buying a can of petrol for? Their motorbikes probably. No, somehow that didn't seem right. She remembered how the Beast had patted it and joked about blowing up Buckingham Palace. People used petrol for making petrol bombs, didn't they? And for starting fires. Was *that* what the gang were up to, then? Were they about to set fire to something—a school, perhaps, or maybe even a house?

'That's really serious,' Tracy thought, more certain than ever that she ought to ring the police. But she still didn't have enough information. How could she report that a group of boys with stripy hair was about to start a fire, when she didn't know where?

She searched her mind for more clues. 'Tweeter's little op,' was the name the Meanie had given it in the shop. That probably meant it had been Peter's idea. Now what would Peter want to set fire to?

'Oh no!' She shot bolt upright, suddenly remembering the picture he'd sent to the clown.

With shaking hands, she pulled the screwed up note out of her pocket and reread it: *'Operation Death Hound brung forward 002 hours.'* Operation Death Hound! And the picture had been of a dog being clubbed to death. 'Oh no! They're planning to attack the Rescue Circus!'

Within seconds she had a pair of jeans and an anorak on over her night-shirt. All she could think of was the clown; of his lovely caravan going up in smoke. Of the all-but-unbearable possibility that he and his dogs might still be inside.

As she charged down the stairs, completely forgetting that she might wake Auntie Nadia, another thought struck her. She ought to ring for the fire brigade before leaving. That way if she reached Carlo's van in time to stop the attack well and good, but if the Knights had already carried out their plan ... if even at this minute flames were beginning to lick towards the van ... what was needed was a team of firemen with hoses to put them out.

She dashed into the kitchen and snatched the phone. 'Remember ... remember,' she told herself. 'Clearly and calmly. Calmly and clearly.'

But something was wrong. Something she hadn't been warned about in Brownies.

'Hello ... Hello ... Hello....' Frantically she pressed the button under the receiver several times.

Still nothing happened. The line was dead. There was no point in dialling the emergency number. She knew already she wouldn't get through.

The telephone wires outside had come down in the wind.

CHAPTER TEN

It was as if some evil power had taken over; a power in league with Peter, the Beast and the Meanie; a power that would whip up storms and tear down telephone wires; that would do everything possible to bring harm to the clown.

Tracy felt it as she raced into the night. She heard it in the fierce persistent hissing of the wind, in the groaning of the cherry trees, in the sudden gloating howl of the gale as she turned from the sheltered path onto the open road. She saw it in the threatening, formless shapes along the hedgerow; but most of all it taunted her from the sky. Gone was the comforting silver glimmer of the moon and in its place an eerie orange glow.

'Too late! Too late!' the glow seemed to howl. 'The van is on fire.'

Of course, until she reached the field beside the Hump, she could not be sure. But how else was this strange sheen upon the clouds to be explained? By streetlamps possibly? Or by some special army helicopter?

'No! A fire! A fire!' the glow continued to howl.

And then, as if that wasn't bad enough, she stumbled over an uneven patch in the road and only just saved herself from falling flat. She would have to slow down, she realised, especially when she reached the lane. With a shiver she remembered how narrow the lane was, with brambles snarling out from the hedge to snatch at her ankles, and no light, apart from that hateful glow, to show her the way.

She felt doubly afraid. Perhaps Carlo wasn't the only one in danger? Perhaps evil power planned to catch her too.

'Turn back! Turn back!' cried the glow.

No. Loyalty to the clown urged her on ... on ... into the lane's narrow black mouth.

If I stick to the middle I should be all right, she thought. But sticking to the middle of anything when you can't see the edges is tricky. The only way she could manage it was by testing the ground ahead with the toes of her right foot before every step. Her pace slowed to a crawl. The glow in the sky seemed brighter and more taunting than ever and there was a sour smell in the air. Smoke? Oh, she hoped not. If only she could move faster, get there sooner....

And then she saw the light. A small yellow twinkle in the distance moving towards her. A bicycle lamp? She pressed herself into the bushy side of the hedge, ignoring the catch and tear of bramble thorns against her jeans. For a couple of seconds the wind dropped and she had her explanation. She heard footsteps, rapid running footsteps. The twinkle was the light of a torch.

Her heart leaped with relief. Who else could it be but the clown? He was safe. At this very moment his dogs were probably chasing the Red Branch gang across the Hump, ferociously snapping at their heels. And serve them right!

'Carlo! Carlo! I'm here,' she called excitedly, forgetting all about the danger of tripping in her desire to give him a hug.

If she had been as Wide Awake as a Brownie Sixer ought to be, she might have noticed that the footsteps were light not heavy; that the runner was neither broad nor tall.

But such was her delight, she noticed nothing until she dashed into the circle of the torchlight and found herself staring Peter in the face.

'Oh no!' she gasped, her arms dropping limply to her sides.

'Tracy!' He sounded as taken aback as she was. 'I was going to call you!' He grabbed her elbow. 'Look, there isn't a minute to lose. We've got to get back to the house and ring for the fire brigade.'

The words jangled like alarm bells in her ears. 'Why? Is the clown's van on fire? Is that what you mean?'

His guilty nervous shrug said it all.

'You pig!' she half-sobbed.

'There's no time to lose,' he urged her forward.

'What's the good of ringing?' She tore herself free. 'We won't get through.'

'How do you know?'

Despite the fact that she didn't want to stand within a million miles of her cousin after what he had done, the only way she could make herself heard above the wind was by staying at his side.

'Because I've already tried. The lines are down,' she almost spat in his ear.

'Yes, but the call-box at the petrol station might be working.'

For a moment she hesitated, puzzled. Why was he so anxious to help? Ah, suddenly she guessed the reason. His suggestion must be a trap. He didn't intend to ring any fire brigade. He was just trying to persuade her to come with him so he could hand her over to the rest of the gang.

Quick as a flash she yanked the torch from his hand and broke into a run. 'Go back to your rotten leaders,' she called over her shoulder. 'You can't fool me.'

'Wait! Tracy! Come back!' She heard his first feeble shouts of surprise. But she was moving speedily now, while he could only stumble along behind and within seconds his sneaky protests had been carried away by the storm.

At the bottom of the lane she turned left, heading for the field opposite the Hump. The smell of smoke grew stronger with every step. She lengthened her stride, picturing the caravan as she had last seen it, cosy and solid beneath the cool radiance of the sun. How horribly things had changed! With a shudder, she imagined it as it might be now—at the centre of a huge orange bonfire with hungry ruth-less flames eating it up. More than ever she wanted to be with the clown, to hear his voice and see his slow gentle smile (although he wouldn't smile in the middle of an emergency naturally). But if she were there, she could advise him. She knew all about emergencies. She knew about cuts and nose-bleeds and minor burns too, which would probably come in handy. And she wanted to tell him what a pig Peter was. Of course he would have worked that out for himself by now. He would know who was to blame for the fire. Just as long as he was all right; just as long as the blaze hadn't got him.

Pale-faced yet determined, Tracy arrived at the site—only to realise there was no way she could rush in and help. It was as if a billowing barricade of smoke had been erected round the field, hiding everything from view. The caravan, she supposed, must be somewhere in the middle, but by the look of things it would take firemen with breathing equip-ment to get anywhere near it. Still—she squeezed in under the railings, holding her anorak across her nose (the way she'd seen on telly)—she had to try.

'This is useless!' she gasped a few seconds later. It felt like struggling through a bowlful of porridge. Gluey lumps had clogged up her eyes and nose and were stinging the back of her throat. If she went any further she would suffocate.

Was it her imagination, or did she hear a cackle above the smoke, as coughing and spluttering, she made for the clearer air outside the gate?

She collapsed in a huddle, her head between her knees, overcome by a wave of 'if onlys': if only she had guessed earlier what the Knights were up to, if only she could have done something to prevent it, if only she could be sure now that the clown wasn't still in his van, trapped at the centre of the smoke. 'Oh, Carlo ... Carlo ... Carlo ...' she rocked backwards and forwards repeating his name.

Mid-rock she felt a hand on her shoulder.

'Carlo?'

For a second glorious moment she thought he was safe.

She looked up only to have her hopes dashed once more.

'Go away! Go away! *Go away!*' she screamed into Peter's unwelcome face.

'I'm here to help,' he yelled back. 'You want to find the clown, don't you?'

She stared bleakly into the smoke-shrouded field, blinking back tears.

'He isn't in there, if that's what you're worried about. He got out of the van the minute the fire started,' the boy said gruffly.

The wind had dropped. Suddenly they could speak to each other without shouting.

'I hope you're proud of yourself and your rotten gang,' Tracy sniffed.

'No. I'm not,' he replied, more gruffly still. 'I'm really sorry.'

'Being sorry doesn't change things.' She sounded just like Auntie Nadia.

In the rapidly dimming light of the torch her cousin's lips tightened.

'Tracy, I really *did* want to speak to the clown.'

So that was it! That was the reason he was sorry! Not because he had set fire to the clown's van, but because he still wanted to get in touch with his father, and was afraid he'd lost his chance.

'Well the clown won't want to speak to you. Not now.' Her voice was filled with scorn. 'So you might as well go back to your stupid headquarters.'

'But what if he needs help?'

'He won't want help from the likes of you.'

The torch in her hand flickered and went out. She shook it. For another few seconds the watery beam shone upwards, illuminating Peter's tight-lipped frown. And then they were in blackness.

He sighed heavily and sat down.

'Peter! Listen! What's that?' Tracy grabbed his shoulder. (Even a pig of a cousin is better than no one, when you think you're about to be attacked by a prowling ghost.)

Someone or something was padding across the road—a bulky panting mass.

'A dog probably.' His voice was subdued but unconcerned.

And he was right. What's more, she recognised that particular gangly shape. 'It's Goliath,' she squealed.

At the sound of his name, the animal whined and bounded towards them, ending up with his front paws on Tracy's shoulders, slobbering a joyful greeting round her face.

'Clever boy. Oh, clever boy. You've brought your master to me.' Surely this time the clown couldn't be far behind! Eagerly she strained forward. Goliath swept his tongue from under her chin to the back of her ear in one last generous lick, then started sniffing round Peter's ankles.

Tracy grew impatient. 'Where is he?' she muttered.

At the same moment the mongrel completed his doggy inspection of her cousin's feet, bounded out into the centre of the road, and gave a short, commanding bark. Then, as if disgusted by their lack of action, he came over and tugged at Peter's sleeve.

'Looks like he wants us to go with him,' Peter observed.

Tracy pouted. The last thing she wanted to do was go anywhere with her cousin, but Goliath didn't seem to be giving her any choice. He was bounding backwards and forwards now, still tugging at Peter's sleeve. Couldn't he sense that those arms had betrayed his master?

'Come on, Tracy.' Their owner stood up and placed one treacherous hand on the dog's collar.

Reluctantly she joined him. 'The clown won't want to see *you*,' she muttered under her breath.

They set off in silence, slowly and carefully, on either side of the big padding dog, across the road and under a set of railings. Soon they were mounting the bank which surrounded the ditch which, in turn, surrounded the Hump.

At the top of the slope, without saying a word to Peter, Tracy sat down. She had decided that the best way to negotiate the slippery downhill stage was on all fours. Sliding and scrambling she reached the bottom of the ditch, where she lay for a moment, regaining her breath.

'Tired?' Peter joined her. 'You could always stay here for a bit.'

'And let you go off on your own with Goliath? No way!' She leaped to her feet. 'You won't catch me playing along with any more of your sneaky schemes. Not now. Not ever. And don't try and tell me I'm walking too slowly because I'm walking every bit as fast as you.'

'It isn't that.' His tone was apologetic. 'It's just ... well ... we're heading for the quarry.'

'So?'

'So I just thought it might be better for me to go ahead to ... well ... check.'

'How do you mean *check*?'

He sighed and tightened his grip on Goliath's collar. 'Oh, I don't know. Probably nothing. Forget it.'

'Forget it! Forget what? Are you planning to push the clown over the edge?' Tracy shrieked.

He stopped dead. 'Just what do you think I am? Some sort of monster?'

She gulped. 'Yes. You're all monsters, you and the Beast and the Meanie. Mean, beastly monsters, all of you.'

For a moment he seemed to hesitate. Then he said soberly, 'The only reason I want you to wait is because I'm afraid there's been an accident. But of course you're right when you say he'd rather see you than me. It's just ... well, I didn't want to upset you.'

It hit her then like a load of Armagh granite. Peter thought the clown had fallen already.

Goliath whined and nudged them with his nose.

'Oh, give over. We ... we'd better hurry,' she said in a small anxious voice.

They pressed on in silence round the side of the Hump and on across the flatter ground to the right. We must be near the edge now, Tracy thought. She tried to remember what it had looked like in daylight. The grass had stopped abruptly. There had been a rusty tumble-down barbed-wire fence. And then the fifty-foot drop into the quarry. She shuddered. Oh, Carlo ... Carlo....

Suddenly she felt Goliath quiver beneath her hand and he shot forward, head down, tail beating furiously from side to side.

There was a chorus of barking below them.

'This is it,' said Peter. 'Go on, Tracy. Give him a shout.'

She cupped a pair of shaking hands round her mouth. 'Carlo,' she called. 'Carlo, can you hear me?'

A pause followed. Then a clear if somewhat faint voice rose up in the distance. 'Tracy. Over here.'

'He's all right!' she cheered. Impatiently she turned to her cousin. 'You can go back now.'

'Yes, OK,' Peter muttered. 'If he's really all right, I will. Just ask him, would you?'

She shrugged and cupped her hands. 'I'm coming, Carlo. Are you OK?'

'Fine,' he called back. 'Apart from my leg.'

'That settles it,' said Peter firmly. 'I'm coming too.'

Bother ... bother ... bother. Tracy felt ready to stamp with annoyance. Now she wouldn't have the clown to herself. She wouldn't get a chance to tell him exactly what had happened without the pig interrupting and spinning him some story to make himself appear in a better light. But wait a minute! She felt in her pocket. Yes, the crumpled piece of paper was still there—the message the Beast and the Meanie had sent him—written proof that he had been involved in the op.

Peter nudged her. 'Try the torch again.'

In spite of everything she had to admit this was a good suggestion. In the time it had taken them to walk from the field to the edge of the quarry, the battery had regained some power—enough to cast a pale glimmering light on the way ahead; enough to guide them to the spot from where the shouts and barks had come; enough to illuminate the figure lying about three metres from the fence, propped against a grassy knoll with Sheba on one side and Ears on the other, and Goliath positioned like a sentinel at his feet.

'Carlo!' Tracy raced towards him.

But her delight faded as soon as she got close enough to shine the torch in his face. She could see his leg must be very sore. In the six hours since he had waved goodbye outside his van, he seemed to have aged ten years.

'Oh Carlo, you're hurt.' She knelt beside him,

wishing it had been a cut or a nose-bleed or even a minor burn (then, at least, she would have known what to do). '*Everything's* gone wrong.'

'Maybe.' He pushed himself up on one elbow and his smile, at least, was just the same. Then, he saw Peter, hovering uncertainly behind her shoulder. To her amazement his smile broadened. To her even greater amazement, he stretched out his hand.

'But this,' his voice boomed with welcome, 'makes it all worth while.'

CHAPTER ELEVEN

Tracy blinked and wondered if she'd heard correctly. What a crazy thing to say! Seeing Peter didn't make up for anything—let alone a mess like this. And how could the clown sound so *cheerful* when his leg hurt and his caravan was burned? The only explanation she could think of was that the smoke had muddled his brain.

'Listen—Carlo,' she spaced her words carefully, the way she did for her grandfather, who was deaf and easily confused. 'I'm—going—back—to—get—help.'

'Oh no you're not,' he replied with ungrandfatherly swiftness. 'One accident is enough in any night. We're all staying put until daylight.'

'But ... but ... that's *hours* away.'

'Just under two.' Peter quietly consulted the luminous dial on his watch.

'Right,' said the clown. 'And I want you to look around for Scruffy before leaving.'

It took a moment for the seriousness of this remark to sink in. 'Isn't he in your pocket?' Tracy cried.

"Fraid not. He belted off across the road when the

fire started. Scared out of his wits. Following the yelps was easy enough at first, but then I went over on my ankle and ... well, anyway, I don't know where he's got to now.'

'We can't just sit here!' Once again Tracy wondered at the clown's calm matter-of-fact tone. Scruffy was his favourite dog after all. And anything might have happened to him.

'We must start looking at once. I mean, he was sick yesterday. He could be even sicker now.'

'I know.' Something in the clown's tone told her that far from being happily muddled he had already done battle with the worst possibilities. 'Still, we'll do no good looking in the dark.'

'At least let me call him,' she pleaded.

When he did not reply, she got up shouting loudly. 'Scruffy! Scruffy! Here boy.'

The cry drew no answering yelp. All that happened was that Sheba and Goliath started to whine.

'Shhh. Easy, lads. We'll find the little fella in the morning.' The clown patted their heads.

'Sorry,' Tracy said as she sat down with a sigh. 'I didn't mean to upset them. I suppose we'll just have to wait after all.'

Waiting. The hardest and biggest part of life, her mum always said—harder than learning 200 spellings, or running twenty miles, or washing all the dishes for a week. And being unhappy and uncomfortable, Tracy now saw, made waiting a million times worse.

Dampness had seeped up from the ground and soaked through the seat of her jeans. Her feet, hands and nose were freezing. She was worried about Scruffy, angry with Peter, impatient to get out of this situation, and scared of what might lie ahead.

She didn't say anything, but somehow the clown seemed to know how she felt. 'Let's close ranks,' he said. 'That's the way to keep warm. Come on, Tracy. Snuggle in close to Sheba. Move in beside them, Peter.'

'There isn't room. Go over to Ears,' Tracy muttered, and to her relief he obliged.

The waiting became more bearable after that. Pressing against Sheba's silky flank, she discovered that a dog's body was as good as an electric blanket, and much more cuddly; that even the darkness didn't seem so black with a smooth, glossy head under her chin.

'All we need now,' Carlo continued cheerily, 'is a *seanchai*.'

'A shona-key?' Tracy had difficulty getting her tongue round the Gaelic word. 'Is that something to eat?'

From the clown's left came a sound somewhere between a snort and a laugh.

'You'd have made yourself very unpopular in Ancient Ireland if you'd eaten one,' Carlo said quickly. '*Seanchais* were travelling story-tellers who journeyed from court to court. And no matter where they went they were welcomed as honoured guests, because their stories kept everyone entertained for hours at a time.'

'Yeh. Well, I suppose we could do with one of those right enough,' Tracy sighed.

'We don't need to look very far.' There was a sly edge to the clown's tone.

The conversation reminded Tracy of the one between the Wise Owl and the girl who went looking for a magical Brownie to help her mother with the housework. She had been told to start being a Brownie herself. But there was no way Tracy intended to start telling stories.

'Sorry, Carlo. I'm definitely not a shona-whatever-you-call-it,' she said firmly.

'No,' the clown agreed. 'But I guarantee your cousin could entertain us from now until the middle of next week. I'm right, aren't I, Peter? It's a long time since I read through Cuchulainn's exploits. But there'll never be a better moment or a more appropriate place than this to hear those tales again.'

'I ... I ... couldn't,' Peter stammered.

'Why not? Tales to raise the spirits and pass the long hours of the night—that's what they're for and that's what we need.'

'Well ... I suppose....' The boy still sounded uncertain. 'For a few minutes anyway.'

Tracy shook her head in amazement. Didn't Carlo realise that asking Peter to tell Cuchulainn stories was as good as inviting a burglar to polish the family silver?

Her cousin cleared his throat and she wondered if she should put her fingers in her ears as a sign of protest. But there didn't seem much point. Her hands, pressed in between Sheba's front paws, had only just begun to warm up, and in the dark he wouldn't have noticed anyway.

'It all began at a wedding feast,' Peter started hesitantly. 'Dechhtire, the King's half-sister, had been pledged in marriage to the Ulster chieftan Sualtam....'

She promptly forgot her determination to think her own thoughts. She was listening. She couldn't help herself. The minutes ticked by. Story followed story, each more vivid and exciting than the last, all woven round King Conchobar and his champion Knight, Cuchulainn—a man so strong, brave, handsome and powerful, he seemed like a god.

But he was human. Peter brought this out right at the beginning when he told them how his hero became a warrior. There had been a prophecy that day. 'If any young man shall take arms today, his name will be greater than any name in Ireland. But his life will be short.'

And eventually, as the druid had foretold, his enemies got the better of him. Somberly Peter explained how, first his weapons, then his charioteer and finally one of his horses had been taken from him through a series of magical strategies. His second horse ran away and he was left, horribly wounded, to die alone on the plain.

'Even then he didn't give up.' The boy's voice rang with defiance. 'Still hurling challenges at his enemies, he dragged himself to a loch where he had a drink and washed himself. Then he tied himself to a pillar so that he was standing up. And though his enemies gathered round in their hundreds, they didn't dare go near him until a raven settled on his shoulder and they knew then that he was dead.'

'Oh!' Tracy's breath came out in a half-sob. She hated sad endings.

'Back in Emain Macha, his soul appeared to the 150 maidens who had loved him,' Peter added quietly. 'They saw him floating in his spirit-chariot, and they heard him chant a song of the Coming of Christ and the Day of Doom.'

The words seemed to hang on the air. For a few moments they sat in silence, staring at the Hump.

'Well done, *Seanchai*,' said the clown. 'You've entertained us royally.'

And looking east across the quarry Tracy saw that Peter had finished his story as the first pale rays of sunlight streaked the clouds.

It was morning, but the surrounding countryside had not yet taken on its natural green and yellow solidity. It remained the same shadowy purple as the sky—as if only half-awake. A breeze hardly strong enough to displace a wisp of hair touched Tracy's face. The waiting was over, yet somehow she didn't want to move.

The rest of the group seemed to feel the same. Noses between paws, the three dogs lay like statues; Peter sat cross-legged, his back to the quarry, his head bent; while Carlo, still propped against the grassy ridge, stared out into the eastern sky.

In the end, he was the one to speak first.

'I always think this is the best time of day,' he said. 'A time of new beginnings.'

The words brought them all to life. Peter's head jerked up. Ears were scratched. Goliath whined and stretched, and Tracy realised that her right leg had turned into a block of wood.

She got up stiffly and tried to wiggle her toes.

'Ouch,' she moaned, as pins and needles began their fiery tingling.

'What's wrong?' Peter asked.

'Everything.' Her leg was coming back to normal, but the heaviness had shifted upwards and now hung like a weight on her heart. The fact that her cousin could tell good stories didn't change her opinion of him one little bit.

She felt this more strongly than ever when the clown tried to get to his feet and fell back, ashen-faced, momentarily shutting his eyes.

'No good.' He had grinned reassuringly before she could speak. 'I'll have to stay here. It's up to you pair to raise the alarm.'

'We've got to look for Scruffy first,' Tracy reminded him.

He sighed. 'Maybe that should wait...'

'No way!' She was horrified that he could even suggest such a thing.

'All right, then,' he conceded. 'You check the mound and Peter can check along the edge of the quarry.

Her cousin nodded vigorously.

'OK,' she agreed, more reluctantly, because she knew she had been given the easier ground.

Still the hint of morning magic lightened her step as she searched through the rough dewy grass. Even in the last ten minutes the sun had grown stronger and spiders' webs glistened from the branches of the scrubby trees which spiked the Hump. 'Fairies' washing,' she had called them as a child. Now they reminded her of a story she had read about a fairy stealing a human baby from its home. Could Scruffy have been stolen, she wondered? After all, if fairies would steal a red-faced squalling baby, how much more might they be attracted to a tiny, well-trained dog?

Of course she didn't believe in fairies. More probably Scruffy had got stuck in a rabbit hole, or been caught in a tangle of brambles.

'Scruffy. Scruffy. Where are you?' Behind her, along the edge of the quarry, Peter's call echoed her own.

She quickened her pace, peering from side to side, studying every inch of ground, not looking up until she reached the top of the mound.

There she froze. Her hands flew to her lips. 'No! No! It can't be.' The shadows must be playing some horrible trick. She shut her eyes. But opening them again, she saw it still, spreading away from her like a long-distance shot on a cinema screen: the slope—the ditch—the bank—the road—and the field, with that awful twisted lump in the middle; Carlo's caravan reduced to a burned-out wreck.

This was a nightmare that would not go away. With a shudder she glanced over her shoulder and saw the clown positioned exactly as she had left him.

For the first time she felt grateful to the Hump for keeping the disaster hidden from view. Poor, poor

Carlo! Down there he looked so shrunken and powerless. Where would he stay? He had never talked of having any relatives. The social services, she supposed, might be able to fix him up somewhere for bed and breakfast. But what landlady would welcome a lodger with four dogs? An even worse thought struck her. What if his dogs were taken from him? They did things like that to people with no means of support.

She turned on her heel and started running back the way she had come. Panting and with a stitch in one side, she reached the group round the stone.

'No sign of the little fella.' The clown set his own calm interpretation upon her sudden return.

'No,' she blurted. 'But I saw your caravan. It's....'

'A write-off.' He finished the sentence for her as if he had known all along.

Worse was to follow.

From the edge of the quarry a muffled clatter of falling gravel announced Peter's return. Eagerly Tracy saw his head and shoulders appear on the other side of the fence. He hauled himself onto the grass. His eyes met hers. But then, instead of responding to their anxious question, he simply sat down and buried his face between his knees.

'Peter, what's wrong? Where's Scruffy?'

His answer came in broken, mumbled gasps. 'Thought it was an old grey scarf caught in the gorse ... wrapped around itself ... and then I saw the eyes ... glazed ... but he hadn't fallen ... no broken bones ... not a mark.'

'A heart-attack,' the clown nodded quietly. 'Poor old fella. The shock was too much.'

'Do you mean ...? No, no he can't be....' Tracy's voice rose to a wail. 'Scruffy can't be dead.'

'Come here, both of you.' Carlo pointed to the grass by his side.

Slowly Peter obeyed, but Tracy stood where she was, tears streaming down her face.

'You needn't worry about burying him. I'll see to that,' Peter said as he brushed the back of his sleeve across his eyes. 'You can pick any spot you like.'

'Thank you, I'd be grateful.'

'Grateful!' The girl's temper blazed. 'How can you talk like that? Your favourite dog is dead. You've lost your van and broken your ankle and it's all his fault. I suppose you're not even going to tell the police. But I will. As soon as I get down from here. I've got a note that *proves* he was to blame.'

No sooner were the words out of her mouth than she felt sorry. Not for Peter, of course, but because she'd shouted at the clown who already looked so sad.

'Show it to me,' he said.

With clammy fingers, she reached into her pocket and pulled out the grimy, crumpled sheet with its misspelt message.

'I didn't know what Operation Death Hound was at first.' Her voice shook as she smoothed it flat on his outstretched palm. 'And then I remembered the picture he sent you. It's what he was planning all along, don't you see? To set fire to your caravan and kill one of your dogs. The smallest, weakest, timidest one.'

'No.' Peter gripped the clown's wrist. 'No, I never wanted that. It was just a threat to scare you off. But ... but things got out of hand. Brian and Martin, they wouldn't wait. Soon as the note came, I tried to warn you. But they got there first.'

'He's lying,' Tracy cried.

Feverishly her cousin shook his head. 'It's the truth. I'm finished with the gang. I made up my mind last night. I got to thinking how my dad would feel. He gave me that book, see—the one about Cuchulainn. Reading those stories and acting them with the gang, I felt closer to him. But deep down I knew he wouldn't like the heavy things the lads were getting into. He'd already warned me—in his last letter before Mum told him not to write. He said he'd made a big mistake in his life. He didn't want me to do the same.'

'So you decided not to take part in the attack, is that it?' the clown asked.

'Yes.'

Tracy clicked her tongue in disbelief.

'But I changed too late,' her cousin continued. Suddenly the energy seemed to drain from him and he sank back onto the ground. 'And I'll be paying for it, just like Dad. Mum's sending me to boarding school.'

For a long moment the clown studied the hunched figure as if he was looking through and beyond it towards something or someone else. Tracy had seen that expression in his eyes once before—the previous evening in the caravan.

Eventually he spoke.

'If you've really quit the gang, your mother might be persuaded to change her mind.'

Peter smiled wanly. 'That's not the way she operates.'

'She doesn't believe in second chances,' added Tracy. And neither do I. At least not for *him*, she implied.

'That *is* a problem,' the clown agreed. But again she sensed that he wasn't accepting it in the normal way. 'We'll just have to trust God to sort it out. I mean. . . .' Thoughtfully he looked from one to the other. 'He would hardly have allowed all this to happen without something special in mind.'

Tracy frowned. It was all very well to say that sort of thing in a tent, or church, or Sunday school, or even in a cosy caravan over a mug of chocolate. But not here. Not now. Not with the caravan in cinders and Scruffy. . . . Angrily she burst out, 'I can't see any rescuing going on.'

He looked at her intently. 'I can.'

Then, instead of explaining, he asked them to help him to his feet.

'It's time . . . to go.' He heaved himself up on one leg, with Peter acting as a crutch under his shoulder. Gingerly he put his injured foot to the ground.

'Better,' he nodded, though his face had gone grey. 'We'll make it to the road.'

Slowly, painfully, they set off, round the side of the mound this time. There was no further conversation. The task of keeping the clown upright over the undulating ground demanded their full attention.

'Stop a minute,' he panted, when at last they reached the top of the bank.

Automatically, from that vantage-point, their eyes were drawn to the blackened wreck at the centre of the field.

Tracy glared at her cousin and clenched her fists.

But an unexpected roar had filled the air. Motorbikes! Her nails dug into her palms. The Beast and the Meanie returning to the scene of the crime! Yes, there they stood, astride their machines in the middle of the road, making victory signs and cheering. And now the Meanie was looking in their direction. He was nudging the Beast and pointing. 'We'll get you, Tweeter,' he yelled at the top of his voice.

Before Tracy had fully taken this in, another figure appeared around the hedgerow, on foot this time. With a furious revving of engines the Red Branch leaders tore past her down the lane.

'Oh help!' Peter muttered under his breath.

'Your mother?' queried the clown.

'Yes.'

Tracy's heart began to thump wildly. What would Auntie Nadia say? If she had been mad before, she would be ready to string them from the rafters now—two smutty-faced scarecrows staggering homeward with an injured clown and three dogs. She must have been worried sick to have come looking for them at six o'clock in the morning.

And now she was approaching: erect, light-footed, her dark hair tumbled around her shoulders like a girl's.

'Peter!' she cried. 'What's happened?' As expected, her voice was sharp with anxiety. But there was another note as well. And as she drew close enough to speak normally, Tracy was completely taken back to read concern rather than anger on her face. She didn't even wrinkle her nose at their appearance.

'There's been an accident,' she summed the situation up before they could explain. 'Your friend has hurt his foot.'

They nodded.

'Better have it checked out at Craigavon Hospital,' she continued in the same gently sympathetic tone. 'If you can make it down to the road, I'll go and fetch the car.'

'I'm really very sorry...' The clown began faintly.

'Don't apologise.' She darted a warm smile over her shoulder as she turned. 'And there's no need to worry about your pets.'

What! Tracy gaped. But this was *unbelievable*.

Auntie Nadia had just invited the dogs back to her house!

CHAPTER TWELVE

'Dear God, what a lot has happened since six o'clock this morning! It's Tracy again, by the way. I expect you're a bit disappointed in me. I haven't had much time for you since my last letter. (Hard to believe that was only twenty-four hours ago!) I had a problem, you see. I just couldn't understand how you could let things happen the way they did. And to the clown, of all people. Someone who really thinks you're the greatest.

'But I'm learning, God. Tonight it looks like you've done a pretty good job around here. OK, I admit it. I've begun to think you're the greatest too.

'I suppose that's why I'm writing—to let you know I've changed. This letter isn't just for you, though, it's for me too—to remind me, next time it seems you've fallen asleep or your attention has been taken up by emergencies in some other galaxy, that you aren't in the business of letting people down—not even someone as grumpy as I am.

'To get back to this morning. As you know, Auntie Nadia took the clown to hospital while Peter and I came home with the dogs. I was still pretty uptight then. Watching Goliath and Co in Auntie Nadia's kitchen was like waiting for a bomb to explode. It was more like a firework display to begin with—just a few paw-marks ... quite a few, really, but no more than you would expect from three mucky dogs on a white-tiled floor. But then Peter decided they looked hungry. We didn't have any dog food, but there was a loaf of bread, two litres of milk, three tins of tomatoes and a dozen eggs in the larder, so he tossed the lot into Auntie Nadia's pressure cooker and put it on the mat. He was right. The dogs *were* hungry. They got so excited they licked the saucepan from one end of the kitchen to the other, slopping all the way. And that was the moment Auntie Nadia chose to arrive home with the clown.

'Her reaction had me in a bigger muddle than ever. Instead of freaking out in a floor-clearing frenzy, she walked calmly through to the hall.

'"Peter," she said, "do you think we could move the spare bed into the living-room?"

'"Sure," says Peter, as casually as if shifting furniture was something he and his mum did every other day.

'So ten minutes later, as well as red and yellow smears all over the kitchen, we had a divan parked between the fireplace and the china cabinet. And all this in the house where up until yesterday you wouldn't have found as much as a curtain ring out of place!

'All of a sudden I began to relax. I saw things had changed, even though I didn't know why. (I still don't, although I'm sure it has something to do with the clown.) The reason Auntie Nadia wanted the spare bed in the living-room was because she'd invited him to stay and she wanted him to be able to see people and rest like the doctor told him at the same time.

'Rest! That's a joke. The only person who has done any resting today is me—which probably explains why I'm wide awake at ten o'clock, while everyone else is asleep. I spent two hours snoozing in the rocking chair this afternoon. Peter and the clown were supposed to do the same, but all they did was talk. Under normal circumstances, Auntie Nadia would probably have gone in and shut them up, but she was talking too—to the fair-haired lady from the church (her name is Elva), who had popped in at lunch-time with a meat pie big enough to feed a farmyard.

'How did she guess we needed it? That's what I kept asking myself. None of us (apart from the dogs) had had breakfast, and people had been calling all morning. By twelve o'clock, as well as me, Auntie Nadia, Peter, the clown and three dogs, there was Jimbo, Elva, the Reverend Entwhistle and two policemen in the living-room. Everyone (apart from the policemen) was starving, but Elva's pie was so big, the helpings just went on and on until even Peter was full.

'Of course our callers hadn't mainly come in search of food. They were there to talk to the clown about the attack. As usual he played the whole thing down, although I noticed how every now and again his hand would stray to his pocket as if he'd forgotten that Scruffy wasn't inside. Those were the times I found it hard to laugh—even at the Reverend Entwhistle's jokes (which are about a million times funnier than Jimbo's).

'The joking all stopped, anyway, when the policemen arrived. They questioned the clown, and me, and Peter (who looked as if he was about to be sick) and then they told us that the Beast and the Meanie had had an accident. Apparently, after we saw them this morning, they went roaring off up the Killylea Road and crashed into the back of a milk lorry. Now they are in Craigavon Hospital with broken ribs and concussion.

'"It's a good thing you got out of that gang when you did, young man," the senior policeman told Peter.

'I expect you know how I feel about the Beast and the Meanie, God. (Apart from anything else it's a relief to hear they won't be scalping anyone for the next few months!) I expect you also know that Carlo plans to visit them in hospital. He wants to invite them to the Rescue Circus as soon as it gets going again. Never gives up, does he?

'Peter and I had a long chat about that after we came upstairs this evening. We were trying to work out what keeps the clown so hopeful—like a cork, always bobbing up on top of the waves. I said it was probably because he thought of other people before himself (that's what Brownies are meant to do), but Peter didn't agree. The important thing, he said, was that the clown had a hero—someone he always expected to come to the rescue.

'For a horrible moment I thought we were talking

about Cuchulainn. (Not that I mind the stories. They're pretty good actually. I was just afraid Peter might be looking for an excuse to start acting them out again.) But it was all right. He'd already discovered that the clown's hero was Jesus, not Cuchulainn. And he doesn't think this is wet. "It stands to reason," he told me. "In a tight corner you can expect a lot more action from a living hero than a dead one."

'I suppose that's something Carlo has shown us over the last twenty-four hours. Like I mentioned before, he doesn't say much, but he has a special way of handling emergencies. You can just sort of sense him believing that you are working things out.

'Well, you'll be pleased to hear that Peter and I plan to try believing this ourselves.

'Just before I left his room to come in here he told me what the clown had told him about his dad.

'"He's getting out of prison pretty soon," Peter said. "Even though he got himself into such a mess, he reckons Jesus can help him start again."

'I knew what he was thinking. I could see the eager hopeful look in his eyes.

'"Mum's different too, isn't she?" he added.

'All I could do was nod, because it felt like if I agreed out loud we might both wake up and find the change in Auntie Nadia was like Cinderella's ball-gown—back to rags at midnight.

'But Peter wasn't letting me get away with that. He looked me straight in the eyes and said, "Tracy, do you believe in miracles?"

'And I said, "Yes."

'I hope you aren't laughing at me, God. I know this is the complete opposite to what I would have said earlier on, when I wanted to go home so badly, and you asked me to stay put. But now it's as if you said no to a selfish little miracle so you could say yes to a far bigger better one. I've been so happy today—playing with the dogs, talking to Peter (we're getting on brilliantly now) and groaning at Jimbo's jokes. I've been useful too. You could have filled a bath with the amount of tea I've made and I overheard Auntie Nadia telling Elva that she didn't know what she'd do without me. Tomorrow I plan to zap them all with my buns.

'There's just a couple of questions niggling in the back of my mind. OK, Auntie Nadia *is* different. It's been fantastic to see her laughing and talking and inviting people in and not minding dog hairs on the carpet. She's really freed up. She even gave Peter a hug at bedtime (she didn't know I was looking). At first he went all stiff and startled and then he looked as pleased as anything and hugged her back.

'What I would like to know is: why? There must be something behind it. Something must have happened between ten o'clock last night, when she tore a strip off me and six o'clock in the morning when she met us on the Hump. Something made her change. But what?

'My other big question is: will it last?

'I suppose you have the answers, God. I'll understand if you don't feel able to share them with me.

Like I said at the beginning of this letter, I'm writing mainly just to say a big thank you for everything you've done so far.

'Yours gratefully, Tracy MacArthur. Amen.'

CHAPTER THIRTEEN

When Tracy had finished her letter, she folded it the same way as all the others and opened her wash-bag. Inside, along with her brush, shampoo and spare facecloth was the soap-box: pink, plastic and ... goodness! This was a shock! The soap-box was empty. Her letters had disappeared.

Mystified, she turned the wash-bag inside out and shook it. No little squares of airmail paper fell out. There was nothing stuck in the lining. The letters seemed to have vanished into thin air. Or could there be some other explanation? Wow! Tracy caught her breath, struck by an astonishing possibility. What if an angel had popped into her room to collect them? She'd just told Peter she believed in miracles, so why not in some sort of heavenly postal system? Angels were often employed to deliver God's messages to people, after all. So what was to stop a delivery service the other way round?

She climbed into bed and lay there thinking this over. It was something she would ask Carlo about in the morning, but in the meantime....

Suddenly her sense of wonder was tinged with embarrassment as she tried to remember exactly what she'd written. Oh dear! At times she hadn't been very polite. If only she had some way of getting in touch with the angelic postperson to let him or her know that there was a final letter to be delivered— one which apologised and set the record straight.

But what was that? She dived underneath the duvet and pulled it over her head. She heard noises—faint but unmistakable. A series of creaks on the stairs. Someone was climbing towards her room. It couldn't be Peter, because his door hadn't opened. It couldn't be a burglar because the dogs hadn't barked. It couldn't be the clown because he was on crutches. Which meant—the girl lay stiller than ever, holding her breath—the angel might be coming back.

The creaking stopped. There was a presence outside her bedroom door. She couldn't hear anything, but she could sense it. Someone was out there, listening, checking that she was asleep, not wanting to frighten or disturb her.

Then came a rustle down low, at floor-level. Again the silence seemed to have ears. Then ... creak ... creak ... creak ... and the presence was gone.

Tracy sat bolt upright and switched on the bed-side lamp.

Sure enough on the lino strip between the bottom of the door and the bedside rug lay a slim white envelope.

She swooped on it like a swallow and darted back to her duvet, tugging it round her shoulders, shivering with excitement.

Imagine! A real live angelically-delivered letter with her name on the front.

What would it say? Dare she even open it?

The spiky second hand of her alarm clock had completed several circles of the clock face before she had plucked up the courage. Cautiously she lifted one corner of the envelope between her finger and thumb; then, reassured that it felt quite normal, she slit it across the top with a hair slide and held it upside down. Three perfectly normal-looking sheets of paper fell out.

She unfolded them and started to read: 'My dear Tracy, I am so grateful for your letters.'

She stopped, her eyes misting over. My dear Tracy! What a relief!

At the same time she noticed the scent—a faint flowery cross between lily-of-the-valley and hyacinth— strangely familiar somehow. It had been around, she now realised, from the moment she had picked up the envelope. Yes, a quick sniff of the white sheets confirmed her impressions. The note-paper was scented. More telling still, she remembered where she had met that scent before. The same delicate flower fragrance had clung to the bed-clothes and curtains in Auntie Nadia's room.

In that moment the girl realised her midnight visitor had been human after all. It was Auntie Nadia who had crept up the stairs. Auntie Nadia who had slipped the envelope under her door. Auntie Nadia who somehow had got hold of her letters—letters in which, quite apart from telling God what she thought of him, she had been even ruder about her aunt and cousin! What was it she had said in the first one? 'My cousin is a bully and a

freak, and my aunt acts like she'd drop off the edge
of the universe if she stepped outside the front
door.'

She squirmed at the memory. Of course Auntie
Nadia had never been meant to see those words. But
somehow they had fallen into her hands. With a sick
sinking feeling the girl turned her attention back
to the perfumed reply, totally confused by its
affectionate greeting. 'My dear Tracy!' There had to
be some mistake. Surely her aunt couldn't be grateful for a load of insults?

It took an anxious scan of the first page to set her
mind at rest. Yes, for some reason Auntie Nadia *was*
grateful. With a sigh of anticipation she settled
down to read her letter properly. Soon she forgot it
was a letter. She could almost hear her aunt speaking, her voice light and bell-like, answering (as if she
had been able to read her niece's mind) the very
questions Tracy wanted to ask:

'My dear Tracy, I am so grateful for your letters.
Of course I know they weren't addressed to me, and
that really I had no right to read them. But I will
come back to that.

'Let me begin where we left off last night when I
lost my temper and turned down your apology. I
don't know whether you had difficulty sleeping
afterwards—I found it impossible. I lay awake
telling myself I had done the right thing; that the
sooner you went home and Peter went to boarding
school, the better it would be for all of us.

'In the end (I suppose it must have been around
five in the morning), I got up and went into the

bathroom to get my sleeping tablets from the bathroom cabinet. I couldn't help noticing your wash-bag sitting on the side of the bath. At the same time I remembered something you had said about hiding money in a soap-box. Did this mean you used your own soap-box as a hiding-place, I wondered? The temptation to check got the better of me. I opened the box—and there were the letters.

'So I read them. Yes, I know it was a dreadful thing to do, but I hope that when you understand how they affected me, you will not be annoyed.

'The thing is, people can sometimes be so taken up with their own unhappiness that they become blind to everything else. They do not see what they are doing to others any more than they see what they are doing to themselves. This is what had happened to me, Tracy, and it took your letters to open my eyes. Reading them, I realised how cold, selfish and bitter I had become.

'Anyway, to cut a long story short I also saw that I had a choice: I could either sell the house and send Peter to boarding school, ignoring what I had learned, or I could aim to change something completely different—myself.

'And here was something else your letters made clear. They showed me I didn't have to do it alone. You know, three years ago when your uncle was sent to prison, I stopped going to church. Of course the Reverend Entwhistle came round to the house, but after the first few visits I refused to answer the door. It was God I was really shutting out. I was so hurt and angry I had made up my mind to have nothing more to do with him.

'But right from the moment you arrived, he seemed to use you to catch my attention—to remind me that he was still there. Tracy, after reading your letters, for the first time in years I prayed—trying to be as honest as you were—asking him for help.

'And the door swung open. It was as if my words had pulled back a huge rusty bolt. By the time I had finished I knew things would never be the same.

'I looked at my watch then, and it was half-past five. An hour when any sensible person would be in bed. But I felt I *had* to tell someone what had happened, and the only person I could think of was your friend, the clown. So I went back to my room and dressed. Then, with the same bubbly feeling I had had as a little girl sneaking out with your mother for an early-morning picnic, I left the house.

'The rest of the story you know already. It's been amazing, hasn't it? Our meeting on the hill. One surprise after another from then on. So many visitors. So much to decide. Of course I know this is only the beginning and many more decisions lie ahead, but I want to let you into a couple of secrets—things I think you will be glad to hear.

'Peter and I have had a chat. It was good. For the first time he talked to me like a fourteen-year-old boy and not like a warrior hero. We sorted out the school business. He's staying at home. In fact he told me that he and Jimbo plan to volunteer as tourist guides next summer when the development of Navan Fort gets underway. He's sure the developers will be impressed by someone who knows as much as he does about Cuchulainn.

'We did not have time to talk about his dad, but I think he guesses my attitude has changed. As soon as the clown is well enough, I have asked him to arrange a prison visit, and in the meantime I intend to write Joe a letter. Yes, I know I told you I didn't believe in second chances, but being given one myself has made all the difference.

'I still can't quite get over the part the clown has played; the fact that only three months ago Joe had talked to him, and next thing (without ever having found out our address) he finds his way to our doorstep. As you said in your letters, he is someone very special.

'Actually the Reverend Entwhistle and Jimbo have cooked up a little surprise for him. He's going to be presented with a new caravan and a puppy. The caravan is a gift from the church. The puppy was Jimbo's idea. Apparently his grandmother's beagle ran off with a corgi so it's a sporty little thing with short legs—ideal material, according to Jimbo, for the Rescue Circus.

'I suspect no dog will ever take Scruffy's place, but I said "yes" to the puppy because it just might fill the empty space in Carlo's pocket, and if not, I know Peter has always wanted a pet.

'So that leaves me with one last thing to say, Tracy—something I've deliberately put off mentioning till the end. As I told you last night, you have been invited to stay with relations in Glasgow until your parents get back. For my part, I would be *very* sorry to see you go (naturally there is no question of my sending you away), but the choice is yours. I know you have been unhappy here, and I understand why. Whatever you decide I shall write and tell your mum how helpful you have been.

'In the meantime sleep tight.

'Good night and God Bless, from your loving Auntie Nadia.

'PS I have held on to your letters. Rereading them should stop me slipping back into my old ways. I hope you don't mind. A N.'

Tracy's eyes were shining. Carefully she refolded her aunt's letter and put it back in its scented envelope. Then, for a moment, she hugged the envelope tight against her chest. She hopped out of bed and went over to the desk. Moonlight streamed in through the window. On the other side of the pane, the Hump was frosted with silver. She lifted her pen and started to write.

'Dear Auntie Nadia, Your letter was the greatest! Today has been the best day of my life. You are my favourite aunt and Peter is my favourite cousin (I know I don't have any others, but even if I did, it wouldn't make any difference). I wouldn't want to go home now if you paid me. I want to stay here and make buns and help with the new puppy. (I think Bouncer would be a good name—like the dog in *Neighbours*.) Actually, if I take a full share in looking after a pet for three months I can get my Brownie Animal Lover Badge. I know I only have three weeks left in Ireland, but I could always come back next year for the whole summer. Maybe Uncle Joe will be home then if the second chance works out OK. I hope so. Also I would like to help the clown fix up his new caravan. Probably Peter and Jimbo and me should sleep in it until his leg is better. What do you think?

'I have lots of other ideas, but I think I will finish off now because it is very late and I don't want to sleep in tomorrow. I want to push this under your bedroom door first thing so that you know that I am staying (and coming back).

'I am also sending you my last letter to God. You can keep it and the others as long as you like. Earlier I expected an angel to deliver them, but now I think God has X-ray eyes. As well as that it seems like he runs the biggest Rescue Circus in the world. I'm glad to be in it. Bet you are too.

'Tons of love, Tracy.'

Escape From The Darkness

by Connie Griffith

Muniamma's heart was heavy as she thought back over the past year. So much had happened. The flood had started it, sweeping away her home and family. Sparky, her dog, was all she had left.

And then there was Kali, the goddess that had more to do with fear than love. How could Muniamma get away from her?

Now she was ill, so Grandmorhter was going to take her to the temple. But it was not from that strange place that healing was going to come.

CONNIE GRIFFITH weaves events that have actually happened into an exciting and at times moving narrative for children. She lives in North Carolina with her husband—the executive director of the American Council of the AEF—and their two daughters. For eight years they were AEF missionaries in South Africa, where this story is set.

K
Kingsway Publications

Hostage Of The Sea

by Cherith Baldry

They came from over the sea, a nation of warriors intent on spreading their empire. When they descended upon a small kingdom that served the God of peace, the battle was short. And Aurion, the peaceful King's son, was the ideal hostage to secure victory.

Coming to the fearsome land of Tar-Askar, Aurion meets the strong and proud son of the warrior king. A most unlikely friendship develops—a bond of love that will prove a greater threat to the Tar-Askan empire than the weapons of war.

Also by **CHERITH BALDRY** in the *Stories of the Six Worlds: The Book and the Phoenix.*

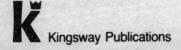

Kingsway Publications

The Will Of Dargan

by Phil Allcock

Trouble has darkened the skies of the Realm: the Golden Sceptre crafted by the hands of Elsinoth the Mighty has been stolen. Courageous twins, Kess and Linnil, team up with an assorted company of elves and crafters—and set out to find it.

Their journey takes them through rugged mountains, gentle valleys and wild woods to the grim stronghold of Dargan the Bitter. Will they win back the Sceptre? The answer depends on their courage, friendship and trust.

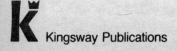
Kingsway Publications